Murder Most Senior

Victoria Fitzgerald

iUniverse, Inc.
New York   Bloomington

This is a work of fiction. All of the characters, names, incidents,
organizations, and dialogue in this novel are either the products
of the author's imagination or are used fictitiously.

iUniverse books may be ordered through booksellers or by contacting:

iUniverse
1663 Liberty Drive
Bloomington, IN 47403
www.iuniverse.com
1-800-Authors (1-800-288-4677)

Because of the dynamic nature of the Internet, any Web addresses or links
contained in this book may have changed since publication and may no longer be
valid. The views expressed in this work are solely those of the author and do not
necessarily reflect the views of the publisher, and the publisher hereby disclaims
any responsibility for them.

ISBN: 978-1-4401-7933-4 (sc)
ISBN: 978-1-4401-7931-0 (dj)
ISBN: 978-1-4401-7932-7 (ebook)

Printed in the United States of America

iUniverse rev. date: 9/25/09

Contents

Chapter One 1

Chapter Two 8

Chapter Three 11

Chapter Four 17

Chapter Five 22

Chapter Six 24

Chapter Seven 27

Chapter Eight 33

Chapter Nine 39

Chapter Ten 43

Chapter Eleven 47

Chapter Twelve 53

Chapter Thirteen 57

Chapter Fourteen 62

Chapter Fifteen 65

Chapter Sixteen 70

Chapter Seventeen 75

Chapter Eighteen 79

Chapter Nineteen 85

Chapter Twenty 89

Chapter Twenty One 97

Chapter Twenty Two 102

Chapter Twenty Three. 108

Chapter Twenty Four. 119

Chapter Twenty Five 122

Chapter Twenty Six 128

Chapter Twenty Seven. 130

Chapter Twenty Eight 134

Chapter Twenty Nine 140

Chapter One

Nobody wakes up thinking: *Today I believe I'll try to revive a murder victim.* Beverly Clavel was no exception. It was an ordinary day, but that was about to change. That morning she was greeted by a pair of beautiful brown eyes.

"Move over, you big bed hog," she said, but the object of her affection didn't budge, but instead stretched out, making himself even larger. She reached over and pounded the snooze button on her alarm clock.

"Ten more minutes," she mumbled. The brown eyes slowly closed, contented.

I've got to stop letting that mangy dog on my bed, she thought, trying to roll over before she realized that she didn't have any room left.

"Might as well get up," she sighed, looking at Scout, the sleepy black-lab mix she'd rescued from the Humane Society two months ago. Scout's arrival coincided nicely with her husband's departure. With each passing day, Beverly realized that Scout was the better companion.

"You won't leave me for a younger model, will you boy?" She scratched under his chin as she extracted herself from the bed. Her feet hit the floor with a thump. Scout wasted no time scurrying over to her vacated spot.

"Scout, you're such an opportunist." The phone jangled, and Beverly picked it up.

"You better have a good reason to wake me up at this ungodly hour," she said into the phone.

"Mrs. Clavel?" a raspy voice asked.

She straightened, not recognizing the voice. "This is she," she said politely, as her mother taught her.

"This is Jane, legal secretary from Bowker and Bowker. Your husband would like to meet with you for mediation tomorrow at two p.m. at our office. Is that acceptable?"

"No, it's not acceptable. I don't want mediation. I want to divorce that SOB."

"Now, no need to get upset," Jane said. Beverly imagined Jane as a prissy legal secretary, with a white lace blouse buttoned all the way to the top.

"And I haven't hired my lawyer yet, so if that jerk thinks he can get away with stealing what's rightly mine in a mediated settlement, he's got another thing coming," she shouted, slamming the phone down. Scout looked up, alarmed.

"That felt good, Scout," she said, laughing.

Beverly stretched and began her morning routine. As she styled her hair, she noticed that the gray roots were fighting with the brown hair, and the roots were winning. Frowning, she remembered that it was her mother's birthday and she had to pick up something for her since they were having lunch together. She pulled on her clothes and walked to the kitchen. She looked at her espresso machine longingly.

"Oh, I can be a little late," she said to Scout, who had finally gotten out of bed to follow her downstairs to the front door and was waiting to be let out. Knowing that kibble was close at hand, he went only a few paces from the door, peed in two seconds flat, and ran back inside, Scooby Doo nails clicking on the hardwood floors.

Beverly turned on the life-affirming espresso machine and wolfed down a granola bar. Remembering that Herb had hated the noisy machine, she ran it a little longer than usual in his honor.

"Mmmm," she said, pouring the luscious espresso into her port-a-cup and mixing up the mocha. After taking a quick sip, she smiled and said out loud, "It will be a good day today."

After feeding the dog, she ran upstairs, brushed her teeth, and reached into her closet to grab her shoes from the pile. She slipped them on and hustled down the stairs and to the door to the garage.

"Guard the house," she said to Scout, patting his head and shutting the door behind her, leaving Scout in the house.

As she pulled out of her driveway she noticed that the Portland, Oregon, sky was its usual gray, and rain was misting down as she started her five-mile trip to work. While driving out of her picturesque neighborhood with coveted big lawns she said to herself, "It would be over my dead body that Herb gets this car or the beautiful house."

Then she remembered that she needed to call her boss. Normally she started work at about eight o'clock, but she knew she might be a few minutes late. She pulled into the grocery store parking lot and dialed her boss.

"Ford Senior Center, Paul speaking," he answered.

"Hi Paul, it's Beverly. Is it OK if I'm a few minutes late? I have to pick up something."

"That's fine, but the copy machine vendor is coming at nine o'clock and I'd like you be in the meeting. And get here quick as you can because Lois is on the rampage. She's trying to set me up with her granddaughter again. Save me!"

"Maybe if you stop flirting with all the ladies, they'll leave you alone. I'll be there before nine. See you then." She chuckled to herself when she remembered that women at the center were forever trying to fix up Paul with their assorted relatives ("she's gorgeous, and smart as a whip"). Unfortunately for them, Paul was gay and in a committed relationship.

Beverly entered the grocery store and chose an unsentimental card for her mother's birthday and a nice looking plant. She loved her mother, but sometimes she had a hard time liking her. As an afterthought, Beverly went to the produce section to grab an apple. Her hand slipped and toppled over the apples, causing the produce guy to rush over.

"I'm so sorry about that," Beverly said, trying to regain her composure.

"It's OK lady," he said. Beverly also heard him mutter, "Crazy lady," under his breath.

After she checked out, she drove to her job at the senior center. As she pulled up, she sighed as she saw the familiar building. She remembered that it had been converted from a grammar school that had been built in the 1930s. It was a beautiful, old, red-brick building, one story, not too large. Because of the changing population patterns, the school was closed. Then the building was refurbished and reopened as a senior center. She smiled as she saw the flowers that several of the seniors lovingly cared for at the front of the building. She knew that many of the seniors that visited the centers had moved away from their homes with yards to small apartments that lacked garden space. Beverly felt happy that she started up the "community flower garden" to allow the seniors to enjoy gardening again. The garden was overseen by Clarice, a sprightly eighty-two year old with long, wild hair pulled back in a braid. She often wore dirt-covered gardening clothes and a wide hat to the senior center.

The misty rain had stopped as Beverly got out of her car. She walked up the walkway to the building, passed the flowers, and entered the center. She smelled the strong coffee with relief because she had finished her mocha. She momentarily forgot the usual taste of the coffee that the volunteers or Joe the custodian brewed. She saw many seniors sitting at their regular tables. As she walked toward her office, she answered a wave with,

"Hi Tilly, is that a new dress? It's very becoming," to the small, formidable woman holding court at the first table she went past.

Tilly motioned Beverly to come over. As Beverly approached the table, Tilly shouted at her, "Beverly honey, did you know that you're wearing two different shoes?" With that, many sets of eyes looked to her feet, and the mumbling started.

Feeling horrified, Beverly clenched her teeth and stuttered. "No, I hadn't noticed, and I don't have time to go back home to change."

Tilly looked at her watch, "Well you're so late, I can't see how it would make a difference if you went home."

Beverly said rather loudly, "Thanks for letting me know, Tilly. I'll talk with you later." She heard the musings the tables:

"It's such a shame that Beverly turned fifty and her husband left her, she's such a dear girl," and "She was always so together, I mean, she never would have worn two different shoes before," and "I wonder if he found a younger woman. You know, they always do."

She slunk to her office. She wanted to tell them that she wasn't that upset that Herb had left her, they'd been growing apart for years. But she did worry that her job would barely cover her most basic expenses. The best she could hope for was a good divorce settlement.

Beverly made her way to her office and noticed that Joe the custodian had finally emptied her recycling box, which had been overflowing the day before. She also noticed that he had done a good job of picking up a bunch of pesky packing peanuts that had strayed onto her floor. She made a note to herself to thank him. She'd barely sat down in her office when her boss Paul came rushing in, breathless,

"The copy machine vendor is going to be fifteen minutes early. I have to step out. I just found out. Can you take the meeting?"

"Of course. Relax Paul—how hard can it be? It's not negotiating world peace."

"Beverly, you don't understand." He put his hands on his hips and stared at her, "I've made some very bad copy machine choices in the past. You might not realize it, but copy machines are the lifeblood of the senior centers."

"I'll handle it," she said with a sigh as Paul handed her a page long list of questions.

"This is what I want you to ask. And write down her answers carefully." Beverly looked at him incredulously and took the paper.

"I'll do my best, Paul," she said, stifling a salute as he ran out the door to his next crisis.

If only I could bottle up and sell his nervous energy, I'd make a fortune, she thought.

Shortly thereafter, she met Terri Orton, the copy-machine salesperson in one of the classrooms. Terri was a tall, striking, African-American woman wearing a lovely beige, silk suit. Beverly hoped Terri didn't notice her mismatched shoes.

When she brought out her pad of paper and Paul's list of questions, Beverly saw Terri cringe. "Don't worry, Terri, we'll go through Paul's list quickly so you won't have to cancel the rest of your meetings for the day."

Terri laughed, "Well, I'm glad to hear that. Paul is rather," she paused, "thorough, isn't he?"

Beverly smiled, "Thorough, compulsive—what's the difference?"

They worked through a couple of the questions as Beverly took notes. Then she said, "This may take a while, would you like a cup of coffee, Terri?"

"Sure thing. Cream and sugar please."

"Good choice. The coffee is barely passable without it. I'll be right back."

As Beverly walked over to the kitchen area, she was stopped by Ruth, her friend and a retired divorce attorney. As usual, Beverly thought, Ruth looked impeccable. She had short, glossy hair that belonged in a shampoo advertisement. Her dark brown hair was a slightly different shade than her brown eyes. She was wearing a black pencil skirt, high heels, and a creamy silk blouse. Beverly looked down at her own mismatched shoes and cringed.

"You're not letting that lousy husband of yours try the mediation tactic are you?" Ruth said firmly. "Statistically, the spouse who organizes the mediation gets a better deal in the divorce settlement. Don't let him pull that crap on you."

"It's funny you say that, because his attorney's office just called this morning to try to schedule a mediation session with me."

"They always do." Ruth looked heavenward, then stared directly at Beverly. "Did you stand your ground?"

"I did."

"You're better off. Just get the divorce; you'll get more in the end. Who's your attorney?"

"I don't have one just yet. I'm a little bit afraid of the cost right now."

"Who does he have?" Ruth asked.

"Bowker and Bowker."

"Ohhh, they're tough," Ruth said. "You need to get somebody tougher. Let me think it over. I'll give you some names later today."

"That would be great," Beverly said, stirring sugar and creamer into the two coffees.

"Just don't wear two different shoes to court," Beverly sighed as Ruth stared at her shoes. "I won't. I promise."

As she headed back to Terri, Beverly heard screams echoing down the hallway. Running over, she saw a group of seniors surrounding what looked like a person on the ground. Knowing death was a common occurrence at the senior center, she feared the worst. *Another heart attack? Maybe somebody fell and broke a hip,* she thought. As she got closer, she pushed her way through the crowd.

"What's going on?" she asked, "Please move away."

"It's Joe!" Tilly cried. Joe was the custodian. Beverly looked more closely. She smelled the sickly odor of blood, like at a butcher shop. She stepped back when she saw the knife sticking out of his back and the blood pooling underneath him.

Chapter Two

When the crowd stepped away from the body, Beverly confirmed that it was indeed Joe, sprawled on the floor face down with a knife sticking out of his back. Taking charge, she crouched down and felt a faint pulse on his neck. She looked up at the frightened seniors. Closest to the body was the senior center's most outspoken customer Tilly, right ahead of the elegantly dressed Kat.

"Please move back! Someone call 911!" Beverly yelled, and then when several people got out their phones, she added, "Only one person—you, Pete." Beverly knew that Pete was the most level headed of the group. "Tell them where we are. I'll start CPR."

Beverly saw Pete speak into his phone while Otis, a retired police detective, looked down at her and said, "Beverly, this is a crime scene. You shouldn't move him." His advice came too late to prevent Beverly from pulling the knife out of Joe's back and rolling him over onto his back with a convulse effort, using a strength she didn't know she had.

"He has a pulse!" she said as she started CPR, her own heart pounding. Even though the blood was coming fast and furious and making a bigger mess on the floor, she feverishly kept at the CPR until the ambulance arrived and the Emergency Response Team took over. They worked on Joe tirelessly for a long time, but they finally gave up. They put him on a stretcher and pulled a sheet over his head. The blood seeped through the sheet as they rolled him out to the ambulance. By this time, Beverly noticed that Terri was out in the hall watching with the rest. Beverly was certain that getting an order for a copy machine was the furthest thing from her mind.

Beverly looked down at her hands. They were covered in blood, as was her dress and her mismatched shoes. All the seniors were talking at once. Terri came over and put a comforting arm around Beverly's shoulder. Beverly was shaking.

"You did what you could," Terri said, looking down.

Just then, two police officers arrived on the scene.

The first one that Beverly saw was a bear of a man, over six feet tall, who had to be at least 220 pounds. He had black hair and a mustache and looked to be in his thirties. The other cop was much smaller in stature and looked muscular. He had short gray hair, and Beverly noticed his penetrating green eyes from where she stood. He looked at the people gawking and said, "We need to question everyone, so please don't leave."

He looked over at the community room and saw that it had plenty of tables. "Everyone please move into that room while we examine the crime scene."

Beverly watched the excitement on the faces of the seniors as they walked down the hall. She knew there was no way that anybody would dream of leaving. This was probably the most interesting thing that had happened to them in a very long time. She could see them whispering to one another.

Beverly looked over at the silver-haired police officer and he said, "Why don't you get cleaned up before we talk." Beverly felt sick as she looked down at the blood all over her.

"I'm Officer Swenson, ma'am. This is my partner, Officer Mike Petrovsky. What is your name please? Also, Is there somewhere private where we can talk to people?"

"I'm Beverly Clavel. I'm the Assistant to the Director here at the center. As far as a place to set up, you can use these two classrooms," she said, pointing and heading down the hallway. She opened the door to the first room, which contained four small tables and a small desk at the front.

Officer Petrovsky set down his notebook and said, "I'll set up here, Jim. We can take them one at a time. Ma'am, do you think any of them might leave?"

"Call me Beverly. Leave? Are you kidding? This is probably the most excitement that's been at the senior center since the director tried to teach the seniors salsa dancing." Beverly knew that she was talking nonsense, but it had been a very unusual day. She noticed Officer Swenson smiling,

"My ex-wife got me to do that once. That may be why she's my ex-wife," he said. Officer Petrovsky just looked stone faced.

"Are you the center director? We should probably talk with the director first," Officer Petrovsky said.

"No, and he's not here right now. He had to go to a last-minute meeting this morning. That's why I was meeting with the copy-machine vendor this morning," Beverly replied.

"Is the vendor the tall woman you were talking with? She looked much younger than the rest of the crowd," Officer Swenson said.

"Yes. Her name is Terri Orton, and I met her for the first time today. I don't think she saw anything, though, she didn't come out of our meeting room until after I'd been working on Joe for a while."

Swenson gave directions, "Mike, you go out and find out who found the victim first. Somebody must have seen something. We'll be in the next classroom." With that, Beverly and Officer Swenson walked out.

When they arrived at the classroom, Beverly explained, "This classroom is used for scrap -booking classes taught by a volunteer who owns a scrap-booking business. She's no dummy, she sells more expensive scrap-booking paraphernalia than I ever imagined possible." The officer looked at her blankly.

The tables were clean, and the chairs were uniformly pushed under the tables and set at equal distances. Beverly noticed that the garbage can needed to be emptied. She made a mental note to herself to mention that to Joe the custodian. Then she gulped, and she remembered. She pulled out a chair and collapsed into it.

The officer looked at her kindly. "Would you like to wash up now? I'll wait." Beverly looked down on her hands and saw the dried blood.

"I forgot for a moment. Yes, I'll be right back." She hurried to the restroom down the hall and washed her hands with hot, soapy water, noticing that there was dried blood under her fingernails that she couldn't get out. She looked in the mirror and saw that some of the blood had gotten into her hair and on her face. She washed her face, then broke down and started to cry.

Chapter Three

L ooking in the bathroom mirror, Beverly splashed cold water on her face. Her mascara had streaked down her cheeks, so she washed her face with paper towels to repair the damage. She looked into the reflection of her eyes and vowed to figure out this crime. She knew how frightened and upset her friends at the senior center were and how things wouldn't be the same until the crime was solved.

As she exited the restroom, she saw that Officer Petrovsky's door was closed with three people trying to listen in. There was Marybeth and Sara, two friends in their eighties, who look so alike they could be sisters, along with Jonah, who was the reigning bridge champion. They had their ears pressed up against the door, straining to hear what was being said.

"Marybeth, Jonah, and Sara! What are you doing? Go back to the sitting room. Stop listening in!" Beverly ordered, sounding like a school teacher.

The three scurried away. She heard Marybeth say, "She always spoils our fun."

Beverly stepped into the classroom where Officer Swenson was waiting, and he stood up and pulled out the chair for her. She appreciated the common courtesy.

"Thank you. Now where were we?"

Officer Swenson started, "I first want to ask you a few questions about yourself and the victim and then about what happened today."

"Joe—Joe's the victim."

"And his last name?"

"It's Joe Boulden—Joseph Boulden."

"How long has he worked here?"

"I'll have to check. He was here when I started four years ago."

"And he's the only janitor here?"

"Yes, he does custodial work and light maintenance.

"And your last name and your role here?"

"Clavel...Beverly Clavel. I'm the assistant to the director."

"Assistant director? What does the assistant director do?"

"I'm not technically the assistant director. I would need a degree for that. I'm the assistant to the director. It's a secretarial job. I help the director by scheduling the classrooms, getting instructors, working with the seniors, and coordinating the volunteers."

"And the director's name is?"

"Paul Glass. He's been with the center for two years."

"And where is he today?"

"I'm not sure. He was in earlier today; he gave me a list of questions to ask the copy machine vendor. But then he had to go to an unexpected meeting this morning, so I needed to meet with the vendor by myself. Originally, we were both planning to meet with the vendor," Beverly said.

"When is he expected back?"

"I haven't seen his schedule. It should be on the computer if you'd like me to check. But often he doesn't update the computer calendar. I thought he'd be back by now."

"Let's start at the beginning. Tell me exactly what happened today."

"Well, I came into work a little late because I had to stop and pick up a birthday present for my mother," she looked at him, "I'm having lunch with her today. Oh, I almost forgot!" she said, looking at her watch. "It's O.K., I have time to call her. Anyway, I got in to work at about eight thirty; normally I start at eight. Most of the regulars were already gathered in the sitting room. They usually get here about seven. Many of our seniors are early risers."

"So if you didn't get here until later, who opened up in the morning? The director?"

"No, it was Joe. He gets here early, usually about six thirty. He did his morning duties like cleaning up the classrooms, emptying the garbage cans from yesterday—that type of thing. Then he would unlock the front doors a little before seven. There are always people waiting to be let in."

"So he's the only employee here that early."

"That's right."

"Go on. So you got in this morning about eight thirty. What happened then?"

"Yes. Everything seemed to be in order. I said hi to the seniors—that's what we call our customers—and went to my office. Paul, the director, came into my office and asked me to take the morning's meeting and gave me a list of questions to ask the copy-machine vendor. He went on and on about how important the copy machine was to a senior center." She rolled her eyes. "Then he rushed out the door. A few minutes later, Terri met me in my office, and we went to one of the classrooms." She looked over at the officer. "See, my office is really small. Anyway, we met for a little while in the classroom. Then I asked her if she wanted coffee. I went to the coffee machine and talked with a couple of the seniors, and then I heard screaming."

"What time was that?"

"About nine o'clock I'd say. I ran over in the direction of the screaming, and I saw a crowd of seniors around something on the floor. I thought somebody must have fallen or had a heart attack or something. You know, that's not that uncommon at a senior center. I asked the seniors to move over, and I saw Joe in the hallway, face down, with a knife in his back. It was horrible. There was blood everywhere."

"What did you do then?"

"I felt for a pulse. Then I pulled the knife out of his back so I could turn him over and start CPR. See, all of the employees and some of the seniors and volunteers took a refresher CPR course a few months ago. As employees, we have to be certified in first aid. We try to offer helpful classes here."

"Did he have a pulse?"

"I could feel a weak pulse. I yelled for someone to call 911, and they did. I performed CPR on Joe until the ambulance people came. Then, I got out of the way and left it to the professionals. I watched as they tried to revive him, but they didn't have any luck. After a while, I think they gave up too, and they took him away by ambulance."

"Tell me about Joe. Did you know him well?"

"Not really. We weren't friends or anything. When something needed cleaning up or fixing, I paged him. He was usually pretty responsive, but he took a lot of breaks. He was a heavy smoker, and we don't allow smoking in or near the building." She looked up at him. "You see, a few of our seniors are on oxygen. Anyway, he often would take smoking breaks in his truck—at the far end of the parking lot."

"Do you know his age?"

"I'd have to look at his personnel file. The director would have that locked up in his file cabinet. I'd guess that he was in his early thirties. He seemed like an OK enough guy, and he did a reasonable job. But there's always been something that bothered me about him. He kind of had a sneer on his face, you know, like he thought he was better than you. He pretty much kept to himself."

"Did he have any enemies?"

"I don't think so." She pondered the question, clicking her fingernails against the table, "Wait a minute." She sat up straighter, her fingers still. "I do remember one of the seniors—it was Laura Goldstein—saying that she didn't like Joe."

"Did she say why?"

"She said that he once called her a 'dirty Jew.' Can you believe that? Yes, I almost forgot about that. It was bad. When I found out about that, I told Paul immediately. I'm not positive whether or not he did anything about it, but I would bet he at least talked with Joe, maybe gave him a warning. You'll have to ask Paul about it."

"When did that happen?"

Beverly thought about that, looking at the ceiling. "I think it was about two or three months ago."

"Is Ms. Goldstein here today?"

"Today is Tuesday, right?" He nodded. "Yes, I'm sure she's here. She always comes on Mondays, Tuesdays, and Wednesdays."

Officer Swenson continued write in his little notebook.

"Did you notice anything out of the ordinary this morning when you came in? Anything at all?"

"No, nothing. Aside from the fact that I got in a little late, everything seemed in order."

"Are you and Paul and Joe the only employees here?"

"Yes. Paul, Joe, and I work full time. And we have a group of about ten volunteers who come in and out."

"What about the teachers who come in and teach?"

"Oh, I didn't count them, did I? They don't really work here, but a number of instructors come in on occasion. Usually they teach classes for free since we're part of the Park District. I think they think of it as a community service. Once in a while, we pay them a little bit for their time. Then we also have a couple people who come in once a week to provide entertainment. There's one man, Samuel Dustin, who comes in and plays the piano and conducts a sing-a-long on Friday mornings. The seniors really love him. It's usually very well attended."

"I think I've heard of him. Doesn't he perform around town?"

"Yes, he's a professional musician. His grandmother comes here. I'm sure that's how he learned about the senior center."

"You said there was one other person who entertains."

"Yes, a woman named Kathy Dawes. I almost forgot about her because I was thinking about people who were entertaining." She chuckled. "She's a poet, and she reads her poetry on Mondays."

"A poet?"

"Yes, and she has some very 'interesting' poetry." She rolled her eyes. "Not many people attend her readings, so I usually put her in one of the smaller classrooms. I think she just does it to be able to recite her poetry to a crowd. And a couple times a month we hold a dance."

"Ah."

"So what do I need to do now?" Beverly asked.

"I know you'll want to go home and change, but I would appreciate it if you would stick around until the crime scene investigators finish up."

"Are they here? I didn't see them come in."

"I'll go check. They should be here by now. I spoke with them by phone just before we started our session. And you'll need to go down to the station to get fingerprinted, since your fingerprints are on the knife."

"Oh, I didn't even think of that! Oh my gosh! I'm so sorry. I messed up your investigation, didn't I?"

"You did what you needed to do. You felt a pulse. You were brave to try to resuscitate him. Anyhow, why don't you go back and make sure the seniors don't get in the way of the CSI crew. Here's my card in case you think of anything else, anything at all. Maybe you'll remember a small detail. Please feel free to call me. Thank you very much for your time."

With that, he stood up and shook her hand. His hand felt warm to her cold one.

"OK, I'll be in the sitting area in the front, trying to keep the seniors away from the CSI team."

"We'll be talking with everyone who was here, so please make sure they all stick around until we talk to them."

"Are you kidding? These people have probably called all of their friends and relatives about the excitement. There's no way anyone would leave. This is two months of gossip fodder for them!"

Officer Swenson gave her a crooked smile, "That's what I was afraid of!"

Chapter Four

As Beverly walked back to her office, she remembered she had some gym clothes stowed in her car from back when she'd joined a health club to rid herself of her extra twenty pounds or so. She frowned, thinking she didn't find the time to go to the health club, so she was basically sending them her monthly donation. Now, she just had to remember if her gym clothes were clean. Most likely they were. But first things first. She had to call Paul on his cell phone to let him know what happened.

Just then, she saw a flash of a person running toward her. No need to call Paul, the Drama King had arrived. And she could hear him from across the hall saying, "Oh my god, Beverly! What is going on? There are police cars in the parking lot!"

"It's Joe. He's been killed!"

Paul's mouth made a perfect O. Joe? What—what happened?"

"While you were gone, some seniors found him in the hallway. I heard screams so I ran over. Joe was lying on the floor. He was stabbed in the back. I pulled the knife out …"

"You pulled the knife out?" Paul's hand flew up to his mouth in horror.

"Yes, I had to get him on his back. See, I could still feel a pulse and …"

"So that's blood all over you? I thought you spilled coffee or something. You have blood all over!" and with that, he crumpled down like a rag doll. Beverly scrambled and caught him just in time. She was afraid he would knock his head on the floor, and she'd have two dead bodies on her hands.

Beverly noticed that the blood had dried on her clothes, and they did look a little bit like coffee. Paul quickly came to and looked at Beverly from the floor.

"What happened?" he said, blinking rapidly.

"You fainted. I thought that only happened in movies."

"I've never fainted before in my life," he said, looking up at Beverly. "That was weird. Oh, yes, Joe. Oh no! What are we supposed to do now?"

"Well, there are two police officers in training rooms A and B. They're questioning everyone who was here when the body was found. The guy I was speaking to, Officer Swanson or Swenson or something like that, he said he wanted to see you when you got in. He's in Room B."

They walked over to the classroom, and the door was closed.

"Should we interrupt? Maybe he's questioning a witness," Paul said.

"I don't know if there were any witnesses. I don't think so, but I'm not certain. I'm sure that if we just knock on the door it would be OK. He really wanted to talk with you as soon as you got in. Let's let him know that you're in. I want to go change—I was just going out to the car to get my gym bag."

"OK, I'll let him know I'm here. Go on ahead and get your things."

Beverly walked toward the entrance. She saw that the CSI team had cordoned off the area with yellow police tape. It looked like they were dusting for fingerprints all over. At least it looked that way. That's what they did on the TV shows Beverly watched.

Beverly noticed that many of the seniors were intrigued. Tilly came over with her friend Mary. Beverly could hear them talking.

Tilly said, "Isn't this something? This is just like that show *CSI*, isn't it? I personally don't watch it, you know, a little too graphic for me. But my son talks about it a lot. And, at one time, I wanted to go into that field of work."

Mary countered, "Tilly, I bet you would have been good in that line of work. You always get to the bottom of everything."

Beverly had heard enough. "Get back to the sitting room ladies. There's nothing to see here."

Mary and Tilly headed back to the room with scowls on their faces, only to be replaced by a few other observers wandering over.

Beverly knew that she wouldn't be able to stop the curiosity unless she made an announcement.

As she walked over to the main room, she noticed that there were about twice as many people there as normal. She made an announcement.

"I'm certain that some of you have been called by your friends to come out here where there's some excitement." She noticed that many of the seniors were looking down at their feet guiltily. "But I have to ask anyone who wasn't here this morning before nine o'clock to please leave. The police need to question everyone that was here before and at the time the body was found."

With that, she saw many people shuffling out through the door. She heard Betty, one of the regulars say, "She's mean, and I just wanted to get a closer look."

Roy, a sprightly seventy-five year old with all of his hair countered with "nothing ever happens when I'm here," but at least they were leaving.

Beverly was feeling sad about Joe's death and shocked that he was murdered. She worried about the seniors and how they would react after the novelty was over. She went out the front door behind the exiting crowd and went to her car to grab her gym clothes. It had resumed raining—even harder now, which was all right with her. She just wanted to wash and be clean. She looked up to the sky and let the rain sprinkle on her face. What a mess. She saw the plant on the passenger seat of her car and hit the side of her head trying to get in. She looked at her watch.

"Mother" she mumbled, "I need to call her before she comes out to pick me up."

She grabbed her cell phone and dialed. Her mother picked right up and said, "Hello!"

Beverly could just picture her mother, Vivian: not a hair out of place, makeup carefully applied, clothing perfectly pressed, and everything matched—shoes, belt, and purse.

Beverly looked down at her mismatched shoes and said, "Hi Mom! I'm so sorry, but I have to postpone our lunch."

"But it's my birthday! Why?"

"You're not going to believe this. There's been a murder here at the senior center. There's no way I can get away."

"What???" she screamed, so Beverly moved the phone away from her ear.

"A murder? Was it one of the seniors? Or Paul? Was it a gay hate crime? Who got killed?"

"It was Joe, the custodian. He was stabbed."

"Then I want you out of there right away," her mother insisted. "You may be in danger. There's probably a crazy person, and he's still in there, stalking you."

"Mom, you've seen way too many movies. And there are about five police officers here. I'm not in any danger."

"Then I'm coming there!" and she hung up abruptly, before Beverly could say no.

Beverly knew that her mother liked nothing more than being in the thick of the gossip scene. And this type of thing rarely happened. Beverly knew her mother wouldn't miss it for the world. So Beverly continued her task of gathering her gym bag and took it back inside to the bathroom and changed. She took a quick sniff and realized that, fortunately, the clothes were clean but they weren't very presentable. Although many of the people who worked out at her health club looked like male and female models just off the runway, Beverly knew she wasn't one of them. She was there to work out, not to look good. Maybe after she lost a little weight she would get some new clothes. She put on a pair of grey sweats with a drawstring, a "Race for the Cure" T-Shirt, white socks, and bright green sneakers. It felt good to be out of her grotesque clothes and mismatched shoes, even if the sneakers she'd put on were bright green.

Just as she finished changing, her cell phone rang. "Hello," she said.

"Mom! Are you OK? I heard there was a murder at work!" Beverly smiled into the phone. It was her daughter, Lisa, who lived in Eugene, where she was an accounting student at University of Oregon.

"Did Grandma call you, by any chance?"

"She just did. When did the murder happen? I can't believe it! Nothing exciting ever happens at that boring senior center!"

"It happened just about an hour ago. I swear, my mother can transmit information faster than Western Union."

"Western Union?" she asked, puzzled.

"Telegrams. Never mind, you're probably too young to know about telegrams."

"Oh, I know about them, I read about them in my ancient history class."

"Ha, ha!"

"But seriously Mom, what happened?" Beverly gave Lisa a summary of the events of the morning, leaving out the more gruesome details.

"You tried to save him? Oh Mom, that's so cool. You're really brave! But I don't think I remember Joe."

Beverly tried to pat down her hair as she talked with Lisa.

"Oh wait a minute, Lisa continued, "I think I remember him now. I met him a few years back when I came to visit you at work. I was probably about sixteen or seventeen. I remember him being kind of sleazy. He hit on me once, in a pretty obnoxious way."

"Wow, I'm really hearing an earful about Joe. I don't know what to think. If I'd have known that, I probably wouldn't have tried to save the guy!"

"Mom, I have an appointment to see my guidance counselor. I don't want to be late. I'm glad you're OK. I love you, Bye."

"Bye Honey. I'll talk with you over the weekend." Beverly hung up the phone, musing about how grown up her daughter was. She was reminded of a code she and her husband had devised to help Lisa out if she ever ran into trouble. If Lisa were ever in a place where she didn't want to be, or felt threatened, she was to call either parent and say she was so, so tired and that she needed a nap. That would be their clue to drop everything and go and get her. Beverly wished that Lisa had used the code when Joe was hitting on her. She would have come and punched him out.

I'm going to get to the bottom of this murder, she thought. *Maybe Joe was creepy enough to hit on other young girls too. Maybe he got involved with another young girl, the wrong one, and was rewarded with a knife in his back!*

Chapter Five

Beverly sat at her desk thinking about the murder and tapping her nails on her desktop. Even though it was terrible occurrence, she was excited about the murder. And she was curious about Joe. She had mixed feelings about him. So many signals. She knew that Joe Boulden had a mother who was still alive since he'd mentioned her, and she saw him once with a woman, perhaps a girlfriend. She wanted to talk with his mother and maybe get to the bottom of things. She brought up the internet phone directory on her computer to find her. Fortunately for her, Boulden was not a common name, and she found two. One was Joe, the other was W. Boulden who lived on a street Beverly recognized. She hoped that it was, indeed, Joe's mother. She jotted down her address and phone number and tucked them into her purse. She figured she'd call on her offering her condolences later on.

Later that morning, Beverly was sitting with Paul in his office when her mother barged in.

"Are you both OK? Have you had the place searched? The killer might still be here. Like in a closet or something," Vivian said.

Paul looked stricken, "Do you really think so?"

"Oh Mom, Paul, stop being so dramatic. I'm sure the cops searched all over the place. You have nothing whatsoever to worry about," she said with more confidence than she actually felt.

"OK, well then. That settles it. We can go to lunch. You're not really dressed for our lunch, are you?" she said, looking at Beverly's sweats and t-shirt. "And that's too bad, because I have reservations

at one o'clock at the Hills." The Hills was one of the fanciest restaurants in Portland. It figured her mother wanted to go there. It
was definitely for the country-club set. And Beverly would be, of
course, expected to pay since it was her mother's birthday.

"Mother, I can't just leave here! We just had a murder! The
seniors are upset. We need to talk with them and settle them
down."

Paul said, "You know, Beverly, you should probably go home
and shower and change, have a nice lunch with your mother, and
then go back home for the rest of the day. I can handle this. You've
been through a lot; you must still be in shock."

Beverly looked at Paul pleadingly to help her escape from her
busy-body mother. She knew she had a love/hate relationship with
her mother and felt very guilty about it. But then she remembered
that Paul absolutely adored Vivian and figured he thought he was
doing Beverly a big favor. Then she thought for a moment. Aside
from having to have lunch with her mother, it wasn't a bad idea to
get out of there. She said,

"OK, Paul, I think you're right. Do you want to come home
with me, Mom?"

"No, dear, I think I'll just stay here in the center then meet you
at the restaurant. Maybe I'll talk with some of the seniors. Even
though they're a lot older than me, some of them are quite spry. I'll
just plan on meeting you at one at the Hills."

Beverly looked at her uneasily. Mom was up to something.
And by Paul's grin, he was up to something too.

"And Beverly, you might want to wear your pretty peach dress.
It really hides your tummy. And do something with your hair. I
think it still has blood in it. I guess you can't do anything about the
color given this short notice, but maybe you can wash it and tame
it a little bit."

Beverly rolled her eyes and bit her lip to stop from saying anything. It was her mother's birthday after all. "OK, Mom. I'll see
you at one. And happy birthday," she said, giving her a perfunctory
kiss.

She went to her office to get her purse and thought, *That
woman makes me feel like I'm twelve years old. No wonder Dad died
so young, I'm sure he was just tired of her bossing him around for all
those years.* She grabbed her purse and locked her office.

Chapter Six

Before heading home to change, Beverly decided to pay Joe's mother a condolence call. She went to her car and pulled out the slip of paper with W. Boulden's address on it. She could only hope that it was, in fact, his mother. But she had remembered Joe saying that his mother lived close by. Beverly was certain that the police had seen Mrs. Boulden, as she figured she was Joe's next of kin.

Beverly drove over to the apartment in the rain, parked, and patted down her hair as best as she could to look a little presentable. She went up to the second floor and knocked on the door. She heard barking. A little woman peered out. *She doesn't really look like Joe,* Beverly thought. Mrs. Boulden was visibly upset and pulled back her dog.

"What is it?" She said.

"Mrs. Boulden? You're Joe's mother, right?" When the woman nodded sadly, Beverly continued. "My name is Beverly Clavel. I worked with Joe. I just wanted to stop by and say how very sorry I am for your loss."

With that, Mrs. Boulden broke down and opened the door for Beverly. She said, "Let me put the dog in the back room so we can talk."

Beverly looked around the apartment. There were papers and magazines everywhere, and dirty dishes lying about in front of an old TV set. As Mrs. Boulden returned, Beverly said, "I worked with Joe for many years. We'll miss him. I tried to revive him. It must be awful for you."

"You tried to revive him? Thank you," Mrs. Boulden said, her voice choking. "This is more than awful. He's my only child. And he's always been such a good boy. The police were just here. I think I'm in shock."

"There, there, Mrs. Boulden. Why don't you sit down? You've had quite a terrible day." She said, patting her arm and taking her over to a worn chair.

"Call me Wilma. I don't know what I'll do without him! He came over for dinner every Sunday. I fixed him pot pies. Homemade."

"Those are my favorite. And homemade, that's really something. But did you notice anything different about him? Did you notice any changes, Wilma?"

"That's what those police asked. No, I haven't noticed anything."

"Does Joe live close by?"

The dog continued to whine, but had stopped barking.

"Yes, he lives over in the next set of apartments."

"It must be nice for you having him so close by. I wish my daughter was close by, but she's a few hours away."

Wilma sympathized with that. "Such a shame."

Beverly thought, *I have to get her to open up his apartment. What can I say?* Thinking fast, she said,

"You know, Wilma, last week I gave Joe a copy of a personal document of mine. He asked if I had an example of a certain contract. I'm not sure why he needed it. Anyhow, I'd really like to get the document back if I could. I was wondering if we could check to see if he has it in his apartment. Would that be possible?"

Wilma looked at Beverly, "A contract? He never said anything about a contract. What was it about?

"Well, I'd rather not say. But I'll show it to you if we find it."

Wilma looked at Beverly skeptically, and then looked intrigued. "Really, you'd show it to me?" she said.

"Yes, I would. But I really want to get it back. I don't want anybody else seeing it. I think it has my social security number on the document."

"Well, you wouldn't want that to get out, what with all that identity theft going around. But Joe's apartment is private. He told me that he never wanted me in there. He said it was because he just wasn't as good a housekeeper as me," she smiled. "The police said they wanted to search the apartment later too."

Beverly bit her tongue looking at the messy apartment.

Beverly said, "I understand his feelings and need for privacy. But I would hate for that contract to get into the wrong hands. . Also, you never know, there may be some clues in there that may help us find his killer. Because we want to find his killer. Sometimes the police miss things, you know, that his family or friends may notice."

"Yes, yes, I want to find his killer too. Let me get my keys. You step outside, and I'll let the dog out. I'll be right there," she said.

Beverly walked to the door, brushing off the dog hair from her sweatpants. Every hair showed up on her clothes. When Mrs. Boulden came out of the door she had put on a sweater and a pair of glasses.

"The apartment is over on the other side of the building. Follow me," she said, leading the way.

They walked around the corner, Wilma in front. It had stopped raining, but it was still fairly cloudy outside. They went to a first floor apartment, and Wilma unlocked the door. The first thing that they saw as they walked in the door was a huge, red and black Nazi flag pinned to the wall over the couch.

Chapter Seven

Mrs. Boulden gasped when she saw the Nazi flag in her son's apartment. Beverly stared and then looked around. She saw that Joe's apartment appeared to have the same layout as his mother's, but where her apartment was stuffed with old furniture, his was sparsely furnished. There was a TV tray that appeared to be used as a kitchen table and there were several dirty dishes in the sink. There was an old TV set against the wall with a ragged chair in front of it and a TV tray set up to the side of it. There was a glass ashtray on the TV tray that was overflowing with cigarette butts. The beige paint, which looked to be throughout the place, was dingy, probably from all the cigarette smoke. Beverly continued to look around, pretending to look for the document.

The women walked back to Joe's small bedroom. There was a full-sized mattress on the floor that served as a bed. It was unmade, and it smelled as if the sheets hadn't been washed for a while. In fact, the whole apartment smelled musty and unwashed. The blanket on top of the bed looked to be an unzipped sleeping bag. There was a large combination safe next to the bed.

There were also many books and magazines stacked up near the bed. Adolf Hitler's book *Mein Kampf* was on top. Beverly searched through the magazines. There were many magazines that appeared to be favorites of neo-Nazi groups.

Beverly asked, "Mrs. Boulden, do you have any idea why your son had a safe this size? Did he have any valuable collections or anything like that?"

"I'm very puzzled about everything. The Nazi flag for God's sake! I can't believe this. And a safe. I had no idea," she said, looking dumbfounded.

Beverly carefully searched the rest of the apartment but didn't find anything of particular interest. So she walked the visibly shaken Wilma Boulden back to her apartment. After Mrs. Boulden was safely inside with her dog, Beverly said goodbye and went back to her car. She sat there, stunned, for several minutes, then started the car up.

"I guess you never really know a person," she said out loud and then headed home to change.

Beverly felt much better after she had showered, redone her hair and makeup, and put on a clean dress for her lunch. She now had two matching shoes, and her purse matched her shoes. She knew her mother noticed things like that, and it was, after all, her birthday, so Beverly figured she'd make her happy on her special day. She looked down at her bloody dress and stockings that were in a heap on the floor and promptly balled them up and threw them in the wastebasket. Then, she looked at her shoes, one blue and one black. They were both covered in blood so she tossed them also. She reached down into her dark closet, found their mates, and threw them out too. The blood-stained clothes and shoes nearly filled the whole bathroom wastebasket, so she crammed the items down.

Beverly arrived at the restaurant a little early, so she decided to have a seat at the lounge and have a glass of wine. She figured she'd need it since she was going to have to endure at least an hour with her mother. She sat down on a brown, leather high-backed bar stool and ordered a glass of Oregon Pinot Gris from the stately bartender. She squinted and read his nametag. It said Frank. Then, she remembered reading about him in the newspaper a while back. He had been with the Hills restaurant for thirty-five years, always tending bar. It was an interesting article. He referred to the beautiful mahogany bar as his ship. He said he had the best job in the world because he was the captain of the ship. Prior to tending bar, he was in a middle management position at a large company. He said that he had hassles from the people below him and hassles from the people above him, with no real power to make a difference. So, he switched over to bartending because he couldn't stand all the personnel problems.

He brought over her glass of wine with a smile. "Your wine, Miss."

"Thank you. This is lovely." Beverly replied.

She watched him smile to himself and go back to washing and polishing the glasses and filling orders brought by the wait staff. He truly looked content.

I need to be the captain of my ship, Beverly thought. *How can I do that? I can start by figuring out who killed Joe and making things go back to normal at the center. Yes, that's what I'll do.* She took a couple sips from her wine and saw her mother come in the door. There was a tall, handsome man behind her. Wait a minute! They were talking. Oh, they must know each other, Beverly thought, expecting to see someone like his companion coming up behind him.

Beverly caught her mother's eye and waved. To her surprise they both walked over. Could it be possible that her mother had a date? Now this was very interesting, indeed. Vivian walked over to the bar and gave Beverly a hug and an air kiss.

"Look who I ran into! This is an old friend of mine from the club, Stan Ross. He was planning on eating alone, but I asked him to join us. Stan, this is my daughter Beverly."

She reached out and shook his hand, "Pleased to meet you. I've heard so much about you," he said.

Beverly's danger radar went up immediately. "Pleased to meet you, too," she said warily.

Vivian said quickly, "Let's get our table. I'll ask the maitre d' to add a person to our table." She looked toward the dining room. "It doesn't look too crowded, so it shouldn't be a problem."

Beverly got up. Stan politely pulled the bar stool out from under her. She placed a bill on the bar to pay for her wine and then followed Vivian. She was getting the sneaking suspicion that this was not Vivian's date but an intended date for her. Vivian's wink tipped her off.

Beverly's face turned red. *The nerve of her,* she thought. Deep cleansing breaths, deep cleansing breaths.

The maitre d' led them to a corner table. Vivian shuffled around so that Stan sat in between her and her daughter. After the maitre d' left, Beverly decided to shift into small talk. "Stan, this is one of my mother's favorite restaurants. Do you come here often?"

"Yes, my wife and I come here often."

Beverly thought, worse and worse. My own mother wants me to be a mistress. Does she really think that I can't provide for myself?

"Oh, where is your wife today?" Beverly asked, ignoring her mother's shocked expression.

"I'm so sorry. I'm always doing that. Did I say my wife and I come here often?" When Beverly nodded, he continued, "My wife passed away four months ago." He looked up wistfully. "Sometimes I still can't believe she's gone. I feel like she's on an extended trip, and she'll just walk through our door any time."

Beverly was heartsick. "Oh Stan, I'm so very sorry about your loss," She said. When Stan shrugged, she continued, "Have you ever gone to Ford Senior Center? That's where I work. Every week they have a really wonderful grief-support group."

"Oh, I don't know. I think I'm doing OK."

"Well, if you ever change your mind, it meets on Monday mornings at ten a.m. They meet for about an hour. I think people like to go there for the coffee and muffins just as much as the talk."

"I'll keep it in mind," he looked down.

The waiter came over to the table and took their drink orders. Vivian ordered a Manhattan, and Beverly ordered another Pinot Gris. Stan ordered a scotch and water. Beverly thought about Frank the contented bartender, the captain of the ship. Vivian, needing to take back control of the conversation said, "Stan, I heard that you've decided to retire."

"No, not really. Just semi-retire. My daughter is taking over my business."

Beverly asked as the drinks were delivered, "What type of business are you in?"

"I'm in the funeral business. I own two funeral homes in town, and I'm a silent partner for one in Corvallis." Beverly coughed and covered her mouth.

"I hear that's a good business to be in," Beverly said, glaring at her mother. The lunch went downhill from there. He talked about how much his wife helped him when they were just starting out and how much he missed her. Beverly wondered who did his wife's funeral. She imagined his company probably went all out for that occasion. Beverly felt sorry for him but was very glad when their awkward lunch was over.

Beverly gave her mother her plant and card over dessert. Then she quickly paid the bill and made a hasty retreat to her car, saying that she needed to run some errands. She knew she had to go to the police station to get fingerprinted. She also knew that she didn't want to be reminded that Stan and her mother didn't just run into each other, but instead had this lunch carefully planned.

After she closed the door, she decided to call her dearest friend Laurie. Laurie used to live next door to Beverly when their daughters were young. Laurie's daughter Maddie was a couple years younger than Lisa, so they weren't really friends growing up, but they got along well and Laurie and Beverly counted on each other to help each other out with various volunteer activities and carpooling and such. Beverly remembered when she moved out of the neighborhood and to a more affluent one when Herb was in one of his especially materialistic phases. Laurie and her husband stayed in the old neighborhood.

"Laurie!" Beverly said when she answered the phone. "You'll never believe my day!" and she went on to tell her all about the murder and the embarrassing lunch.

"You poor thing! Murder! CPR! And exactly how old was the guy your mom was trying to set you up with?"

"He had to be seventy-five if he was a day."

"Seventy-five." She said with a laugh "I imagine your mother must have thought she was doing you a big favor."

"And he's in the funeral business." Laurie burst out laughing at that.

"Well, your day's almost over now."

"Right, I just have to stop at the police station to get fingerprinted. My prints are all over the guy. And the murder weapon."

"Never a dull moment, huh?" Laurie said.

"Gotta go, now. I just pulled into the police station. Talk with you later."

"OK. Call me tomorrow; let me know if anything happened."

She closed her phone, and then opened it up again. After rummaging through her purse, she found Officer Jim Swenson's card. She dialed the number. He agreed to meet her at the front door of the precinct. *I can't believe I'm at a police station. What a day,* she thought with a sigh.

Chapter Eight

Beverly sat down in the orange plastic chairs in the waiting area and marveled that she had never before been in a police station. No calls in the middle of the night to bail anyone out, and no crimes committed against her requiring her to go and identify a perp in a lineup. No, her life had been ordinary and uneventful up until this point.

She was startled out of her reverie as she realized Officer Swenson was standing in front of her, trying to get her attention.

"Ms. Clavel?" Officer Swenson had said, "You look deep in thought."

"It's just that I've never been to a police station before," she said, jumping up.

"Oh really, I've been here hundreds of times," he said, smiling.

"Ha! I guess I've led a sheltered life, Officer Swenson."

"Probably a very fortunate life. There aren't a lot of happy stories that happen here. Although, we are always glad when we can catch and arrest the wrongdoers. And by the way, you can call me Jim."

"I'd think being able to catch the bad guys would make things worthwhile," she said.

"Yes. It does. Let's get you fingerprinted first. Follow me please." Beverly followed Jim down the hall to a woman behind a big counter.

"Jesse, this is Beverly Clavel. We need to take her prints."

"Is this regarding the case at the senior center this morning?"

Jim nodded, and then she said, "That was some bad business there. I'm sorry Ma'am. Did you know the victim?"

When Beverly nodded her head, the woman behind the desk frowned. She then pulled out a form. She looked at Beverly, "Please fill out the top part of this form." She clipped the form to a clip-board and gave Beverly a pen. Beverly quickly filled out the form and signed her name.

"Here you go," she said. "And I need to see some ID. May I see your driver's license?"

Beverly dug through her purse and got out her license. The piece of paper with Wilma Boulden's address and phone number fell out. She hastily put it back and produced her license.

"Here you go."

Jesse wrote down some numbers from her license and handed it back to Beverly. Then, she led Beverly over to a flat scanner. She instructed her on how to place her fingers on the scanner one hand at a time. The computer scanned several images as the woman typed in information on the computer. She also took images of her palms. She thanked her, and Beverly went back to Jim.

"We've learned a little bit more about the case. If you have a little time, my partner and I would like to ask you a few more questions," he said.

Beverly said, "That's fine. I want to help in any way in any way that I can."

She felt like she was in a detective movie. She looked around at the dull surroundings. She thought it was kind of like the *Barney Miller* TV show that was on in the seventies or maybe it was the eighties—old, metal desks everywhere and lots of gray. She followed Jim realizing now how attractive he was. She liked the way his slacks fit him from the back and those beautiful green eyes. He seemed hardened, yes, but there seemed to be an underlying kind-ness there—Beverly knew all of this just by looking at his behind. She chuckled to herself, *I'm an excellent judge of character, especially from behind.*

They went up the stairs to the roomful of desks. Beverly rec-ognized Jim's partner, the big burly guy, but didn't remember his name.

"Mike, let's go into the conference room if nobody's there. It's more comfortable in there," Jim said.

"Sure," Mike said, "Ms. Clavel, would you like a cup of cof-fee?"

"Please call me Beverly. I'm not sure if I want a cup of coffee. I heard that police station coffee has a reputation of being miserable. And it is late in the day."

"Well if you like coffee, you've come to the right place," Mike said. "We have a colleague who's a coffee connoisseur. He makes sure we have the best brew. He grinds it himself."

"Then how can I refuse?" Beverly smiled and said, "A little cream and sugar please."

Jim led her to the conference room and pulled her chair out for her. She asked, "Is this a conference room, or is it really an interrogation room? Like they have in those cop shows? Are you and your partner the good cop/bad cop? Which is which?"

He shook his head, "I think you've been watching too many movies. This is just a conference room. And it's a place where many boring meetings take place. But there is a real, true interrogation room downstairs. There's a one way window and the door locks from the outside."

Mike returned with three coffees. Beverly took a sip and sighed.

"You weren't kidding!" she said. "This coffee is great. What a pleasant surprise. Now, tell me what you found out. Maybe I can help you with your investigation."

She caught Mike and Jim looking at each other and rolling their eyes slightly.

"Well, turns out that our victim was struck with a blunt object before he was stabbed." Jim said.

"Do you think the stabbing was done just in case? Like just in case the hit didn't kill him?" Beverly asked, shocked. Then she looked up and said, "And he fell forward probably after he was hit."

"Could be," Jim said, not really committing.

"And even the stabbing didn't work, because I felt a pulse when I checked," she stated.

"That's right," Mike said.

"So that," Beverly said, pointing at him, "shows that our murderer wasn't a professional." She looked at the two officers proudly.

"That's probably right. But another thing came up when the autopsy was being done and we wanted to talk with you about it,"

Jim said as Beverly looked at him. "He had a large tattoo on his back. It was of a Nazi swastika."

"Well, after today, that doesn't surprise me one bit." Jim and Mike looked puzzled.

"You see, I paid a condolence call to his mother today. And she took me over to his apartment. I told her that we could look for clues, you know—to find his killer."

Jim looked at her. "That's not a good idea at all. That was not a safe thing to do."

"It was OK. She had a key. You would be shocked at what we saw! A huge Nazi flag, right when you walk in the door. Then a bunch of neo-Nazi magazines and stuff by his bed. And that Adolf Hitler book, right on top."

"A book about Adolf Hitler, or do you mean *Mein Kampf?* Was that it?" Mike asked.

"*Mein Kampf*, yes, that was it."

"What else did you notice about his apartment?" He asked.

"He had a big safe. Let me tell you, his poor mother was shocked by all of this. Poor thing!" She continued, "I mean, I told you about his calling one of the seniors a 'dirty Jew,' and I just found out that he made a play for my daughter when she was only sixteen or seventeen. That just made me sick. But this Nazi stuff. That's scary. And I worked with him all this time."

Jim said, "So the obvious question is who he ticked off enough to want to kill him? Do you think he might be involved in any group neo-Nazi activities? You know, meetings, rallies?"

"Not that I've noticed. But then again, how would I really know? I just knew him at work. It appears that he had a totally different life after hours."

"Have you ever seen anyone that, say, met him for lunch or something?"

Before answering, Beverly thought for a moment, tapping her fingernails on the table. She stopped tapping and said, "He went to his truck a lot, on smoking breaks and to eat his lunch I assume. You know, they don't allow smoking anywhere near the building. A few of the seniors have oxygen tanks. Once in a while, I would come out to the parking lot to my car, and I was parked in the same general area as his."

She looked up, thinking.

"I saw him talking on the phone a lot. So he must have had some friends or relatives. He just seemed like such a loner. He rarely talked to any of the seniors. And most of them are so friendly, especially to men. You know it's about eighty percent women there. A male friend of mine used to say 'why do men die before their wives?' And everyone would always take the bait and say 'I don't know, why?' and he would say, 'Because they want to.'"

Jim smiled and said, "Eighty percent women, huh?" Beverly nodded.

"Did you ever see the victim with anyone? You know, a friend in his truck or someone who met him?" Mike asked.

"Come to think of it, I do remember seeing him with somebody, but only once. See, he started work before anyone else, real early. So he got off pretty early too, usually about three or three thirty. One day, I had to go out to my car—I'd left something in there that I needed," Beverly said and sipped her coffee.

She continued, "And he had just gotten off work and was walking over to his truck. I said goodbye to him, and he grunted or something. He seemed in a hurry, but I figured he was just glad to be done with work for the day." She looked at the two men and said, "Heaven knows I feel that way sometimes."

She said, "Anyhow, after I got to my car I casually looked over to his truck and there was somebody already in his truck when he got in. And what surprised me even more was that it looked like a woman in there. I didn't get a good look at her, but she looked a little younger than Joe and she had really short black hair."

She opened her eyes wide and said, "And the weird part was that I think half of her head had no hair, like she'd shaved half of it off. And she had enormous earrings. Since she was just sitting there, I have no idea how tall she was or how much she weighed or anything. That's about all I noticed. The hair was unusual."

Jim said, "Did he seem happy to see her?"

"They didn't kiss or anything. In fact, he seemed like he was surprised to see her, even a little angry. Maybe he didn't want to be seen with her or something. He just hopped in the truck and drove off fast. I wondered if she had walked there or took the bus or what. It just seemed a little weird. But the thing that struck me as odd was that he was with anyone at all. I guess people surprise you. He seemed like a real social zero to me."

"Well, I think we still have a lot to learn about Mr. Joe Boulden," Jim said.

Chapter Nine

A fter speaking with the officers, Beverly drove home. Her mind was racing. She took some deep breaths to calm herself. She thought some more about the happy bartender that she remembered seeing just before her lunch with her mother. Captain of his own ship. *What can I do to be like that?* She wondered. *He's happy because he's found something interesting that he enjoys doing. I'd have to find something beside bartending to interest me, though. I couldn't mix a drink to save my life.*

She drove past an old couple walking down the street. She thought about the senior center and the murder.

What did really happen to Joe? I knew him about as well as anyone else. Maybe I can help solve the murder.

As she pulled her silver BMW into the driveway, she heard Scout barking. She hurried inside, and let Scout out via the open garage. She smiled when she thought that he was always so happy to see her. He could barely contain himself, but he did go pee on his favorite bush and then ran back to her with a wagging butt. He didn't just wag his tail when he was happy, he wagged his whole butt. She looked at him and laughed.

"Scout, you're so funny."

She went out to the mailbox. There were mostly bills and lots of mail addressed to Herb. She set it aside to forward to his love nest. Something caught her attention. A postcard addressed to Herb announcing his thirty-fifth high school reunion. *I'm sure he'd love to go and show off his new flame,* she thought. *Ha! They would think it was his daughter.*

She remembered going with him to an earlier high school reunion. Lisa was just five years old, and his parents watched her for the weekend as they took the trip to Chicago. They made a long weekend of it, and stayed at a downtown hotel one night and the rest of the time stayed with his parents in a Northwest suburb. They went to the Art Museum and went walking around and window shopping on the Magnificent Mile. They made love in the fancy hotel and got up and ordered room service. Then they made love again before they had to check out.

What happened to us? she thought.

Herb had grown up in Chicago, and his mother was still there. Beverly realized sadly that she would be losing his family in the divorce. With Lisa nearly grown, there will be little reason for contact. And she and Lisa loved Herb's family, Beverly thought sadly. His mother was sweet, and a wonderful grandma.

She walked upstairs to her bedroom. She took off her dress and hung it up carefully. She took off her nylons, thinking, *Who invented these awful things?* and set them next to the sink to wash them out. She remembered that Lisa never wore nylons, even during wintertime. But in the cold weather, looking at Lisa's bare legs made her shiver. Beverly put on her most comfortable fleece pants and a sweatshirt and crouched down to pet Scout.

"Now I can give you some attention, Boy." She had read that just petting an animal lowers your blood pressure and she believed it. Scout promptly lay down on his back with his legs in the air begging for a belly rub. Beverly complied, and Scout seemed to smile. Every time she stopped petting him, he would whine a little bit and look awfully cute. So, she just lay down on the carpet and rubbed his tummy.

The events of the day came rushing back to her.

"Let's take a little nap, Scout." Even though it was about four o'clock, she crawled under her pink down comforter she bought for herself after Herb left. Scout jumped onto the bed and snuggled in with her. Exhausted, she fell asleep.

She awoke with a start. She dreamed that Herb was sleeping next to her and they had just had sex and she was stabbing him in the back, over and over and over. The blood was going all over her pretty pink comforter. When she woke up, she stifled a scream, and Scout went on high alert. His hackles were raised, and he was looking at the door. He emitted a low growl.

She petted him, "It's OK Scout, I just had a bad dream." After a few minutes, she glanced at the clock. It was nearly dinnertime. She'd been asleep for well over an hour.

"I'll bet you're hungry, Boy. Let's get our lazy butts out of bed."

She slowly swung her legs over the side of the bed and got up. She stretched and looked around her bedroom. She felt good that she had pretty much banished any evidence of Herb. She hadn't painted the boring beige walls yet, but she had the new comforter and she had easily taken over his bureau. She took all of the little things that he had on top of the bureau—cuff links, change, even a couple tie tacks—and put them in a bag and threw them in the garage. She remembered that he had taken a lot of his clothes with him when he left. But about a month ago she realized that she didn't want him back even if he wanted to come back, so she packed up the rest of his stuff and put it in big garbage bags. She informed him that if he didn't come and get his things within two days that she would take the bags to Goodwill. She left them in the garage. After he picked up the bags, she changed the locks and reset the garage-door openers.

Looking around the room, she saw some of her favorite things. On her bureau was a silver mirror and brush that had been her grandmother's. She remembered sleeping over at her grandmother's house in Eastern Oregon. Her grandmother lived on a small farm. She was a hard working farm woman and her only vanity was her hair. Beverly remembered her long, silky silver hair that she usually pulled up into a bun. Beverly remembered that every night she let her hair down and brushed it a hundred times with her silver brush. As a girl, Beverly loved to watch her brush her pretty hair. She wondered now whether her grandmother had been happy. After her husband of fifty years died, she sold the farm for a lot less than it was worth, in Herb's opinion, and moved into the little town that was close to the farm. She had a cute, two-bedroom house and lived the rest of her life tending the most beautiful flower garden in town. She seemed happy. But that had to be a hard life, being a farmer, and not very realistic for Beverly, she thought, thinking again about the happy bartender.

Beverly's eyes rose to the pictures on the wall. Family photos were scattered all over the house. The photos were mostly of Lisa in various stages of growing up. But in Beverly's bedroom most of the pictures were watercolors of landscapes and seascapes—calming colors, some floral paintings. There was also a little reading chair and reading lamp in the corner of the bedroom and a huge picture window looking out on to the backyard. The backyard was large, larger than Beverly preferred, but she and Herb had a gardening service, so there wasn't much to do, especially since Beverly did not enjoy gardening nor had she inherit her grandmother's green thumb. Darn, she thought, another item to add to the financial settlement; there's no reason in the world the yard should have to suffer due to his unfaithfulness.

Shaking herself out of her memories, she decided to work on her own murder investigation. She went into the kitchen and got out a package of note cards that she used to write out recipes. She started writing a chronology the day of the murder, putting names of the people involved at the top of each card. She tried to piece things together, but came up very short. She just didn't have enough information. She set her cards in a row and took a look. She remembered reading about this technique in a few of her mystery novels. It was supposed to uncover holes and questions to pursue.

On Paul Glass' card she wrote, "Gone at time of murder?"

She made a card for Wes Garcia, Paul's partner, with a big question mark on it. She then wrote out a list of things she needed to accomplish soon, including finding and interviewing neighbors of the victim, finding out if he had any friends, and finding out the identity of the girl Beverly had seen in Joe's truck: the girl with one half of her hair shaved off. Was she his girlfriend?

The phone rang and startled her out of her musings. She saw Lisa's cell phone number on her caller ID.

"Hello?" she said.

"It's me, Mom. I just spoke with my guidance counselor. I'm dropping out of school. I'll be home at the end of the week."

Beverly sank to the floor and petted Scout furiously, hoping that it was true that it really would lower her blood pressure.

Chapter Ten

"You're dropping out of school??" Beverly exclaimed to the phone.

"Mom, don't have a fit! I haven't been doing very well this semester," Lisa said.

"Why didn't I know about this? Who's paying your bills young lady?" Beverly cringed as she realized she sounded just like her mother. "Are you flunking out?"

"I guess technically I am flunking out, at least this semester I am. I saw my guidance counselor yesterday. But I look at it more as an opportunity to reflect and take a little time off— you know, to decide what I want to do."

Beverly saw her past flash before her. She had completed exactly one semester of college and decided to "reflect, take some time off." She never went back. Life got in the way first, then marriage and family.

"Lisa. I know I've told you this a hundred times. I've always, always regretted not getting my college degree. You have no idea how hard it is to get a decent job without it, more so now than when I was your age."

"But Mom, I'll be getting my degree, just not right now."

"You had decent grades last semester. What happened?"

"My classes this semester are so much harder. And I'm just not into it."

"Not into it? Do you realize how much your father and I have sacrificed to send you to college? To make this education possible for you was always our number-one priority. And now all I get from you is that you're not into it?" she fumed.

"Mom, this semester is hopeless. I'm flunking every subject. I just need to take a semester off and regroup. I just want to come home. And now with the murder and stuff, and Dad leaving—well, I just want to be home."

"Oh, no, no, no Lisa, don't pin this on us. You didn't flunk out because of what happened today, or yesterday, or two months ago when Dad left. This is about you and your lack of dedication and commitment. I'm so disappointed in you, and so very surprised. What are you thinking?"

"Well there's no sense at all in me staying here. There's no way I can bring my grades up this semester, so I'm coming home."

"Is there something else going on?"

After a slight hesitation, she said, "No, why would you say that?"

"It's just really unlike you; you've always been a good student. I'm just so shocked." Beverly's phone beeped, indicating another call coming in.

"Lisa, I'm so sorry, I've got another call, but I want to talk with you later. We're not done with this conversation."

"OK. But I'm coming home later in the week after I pack up."

"No, let's not make the decision now. Attend your classes today. You darn well better try to salvage this semester, Lisa," and with that Beverly slammed down the phone.

The phone immediately rang. Caller ID let her know that it was her mother calling. *I'm truly not up for this, and she is the very last person I want to talk to,* Beverly thought, reluctantly picking up the phone.

"Beverly, dear." Her mother's grating and high irritating voice sprang into her ear.

"Mother." She said, gritting her teeth.

"What did you think of Stan?"

"What do you mean exactly?"

"I mean, do you think you might like to see him again?"

"Mom, you've got to be joking. He seemed like a nice guy, of course, but he obviously is still grieving his late wife. And I can't believe you tried to fix me up. And with that old guy. And Herb just left a couple months ago!" She said, petting Scout furiously. Scout looked up at her in surprise.

"Well honey, at my age, I know when I see a good thing. A new widower doesn't come along very often. And he seems quite smitten with you I must say."

"Smitten! Mother, how could you? He must be at least twenty-five years older than me!"

"Dear, you're not getting any younger. You were in your twenties when you married Herb. Things are a lot different now. Have you looked in the mirror lately? It's only the older men that are looking for people like you."

"Mom, if you like him so much, why don't you go after him? He's closer to your age. This conversation is OVER!" she said and slammed the phone down.

Beverly slunk down on the floor.

"Scout, I haven't fed you yet, have I?"

She got up and went over to his kibble container, took out a few scoops, and put it in his bowl. She made him sit, and then let him at it. While he was chowing down, she dumped and re-filled his water bowl and set it down. Normally, she waited to feed him until after she had eaten (after all, that's what the dog manuals said—maintaining that you are top dog and all), but Beverly knew that he'd been so patient and had missed his normal feeding time.

She walked over to the refrigerator and looked inside. She pulled out a container of yogurt, grabbed a spoon and a glass of water, and sat down with the newspaper that she hadn't had a chance to read. On the front page of the community section was a picture of Paul's partner, Wes Garcia. He was smiling broadly. It was some sort of dedication of a building that he had recently redeveloped. Not surprisingly, it was in the Pearl District, an upscale area of Portland. He had been interviewed and talked about some of the projects that he was currently working on, including some redevelopment of some public-housing units. It was a controversial project, with many sides weighing in. It seemed odd to her that Wes and Paul were together. They just seemed so different. While Paul was certainly a dedicated worker at the center, he wasn't particularly driven like this guy, and Paul was obviously gay, while Wes was still in the closet and kept his relationship with Paul a secret.

Beverly wondered why, in this day and age, in this liberal town, Wes still kept his homosexuality a secret. True, he was quite a bit older than Paul, but still! The only reason Beverly knew about their relationship was because Paul told her in confidence and had her over for dinner (with him and Wes). Even though Paul and Wes lived together in the Pearl District, they maintained separate phone lines. And they had a special doorway in the building and a private penthouse elevator toward the back of the building. But Beverly smiled when she thought about Paul. He was very charming and very young and good looking. Beverly was certain that there was affection on both sides.

"I'm sure there will be some press about the murder in tomorrow's paper." She said to Scout, who was by her side, hoping for something—anything—to drop on the floor. She finished her yogurt, rinsed out the container, and stuck it in her recycling bin. She grabbed Scout's leash and took him for a short walk around the neighborhood. It was dark, and Beverly hoped they wouldn't run into a coyote. They were known to frequent the neighborhood, mostly looking for little dogs and cats for dinner. She remembered a friend mentioning that her cat had a little bell on her collar, and Beverly thought that it would serve as a nice dinner bell for a hungry coyote.

"I'm glad you're a big dog, Scout. No coyote's going to mess with you!"

They finished their walk, and Beverly went up to bed. She pulled off her clothes, put on her most comfortable nightgown, and slipped under her sheets. She set the alarm for her regular time, but then thought, *I wonder if the senior center will be open? Oh, unless Paul's thinking about it, there will be nobody there to open up the building tomorrow.* She reset her alarm for an hour earlier and closed her eyes.

The moment she closed her eyes, she had visions of Joe's bloody body and of pulling the knife out of his back again and again and again. She saw the faces of the seniors as they watched in horror as she tried to revive Joe. When it was happening, she was so focused on her task that she didn't even notice the seniors crowding around. She visualized the blood on her hands and clothes. She tried to do some mind-clearing exercises that she'd learned in yoga classes—deep cleansing breaths. Finally, exhaustion took over and she fell asleep wondering, *How do those police get any sleep at all?*

Chapter Eleven

Beverly was enjoying a slow dance with George Clooney when she was rudely interrupted by the alarm clock playing an old Elton John song. She looked at the time and figured she must have made a mistake in setting the alarm time last night. It was soooo early! But then, the events of the previous day came rushing back, and she knew she had to get up and face the day. She could hear the rain outside tapping on the windows.

Scout was hogging the bed. She pushed him over, and he groaned. She was reminded of the many nights when Lisa would snuggle up in between her parents after a nightmare. She remembered staying up to listen to her smooth breathing. It was so satisfying to be able to make it all better. But she couldn't make it all better anymore. Unfortunately, she knew that Lisa had to make her own mistakes, and by dropping out of school, she was making a major-league one.

Although it felt so good under her warm comforter, Beverly knew she had to get up to open up the senior center this morning. Pondering what had happened, she dragged herself out of bed and started the shower. While the water warmed up, she looked in the mirror. Her hair was sticking out in every which way, and she still was in desperate need of a touchup. *But no time for that this morning*, she thought, as she jumped in the now steamy shower.

What am I missing? She thought. *I'm sure the seniors must know a lot that I don't know about. They know everything. I just need to pay more attention.*

Feeling better after her shower, she toweled off and looked in her closet for something to wear. She chose a pair of black pants, a black shell top, and a colorful jacket to go over it. She combed out her hair a little bit, and decided to mousse it rather than attempt to dry and straighten it. Then she applied her makeup and went downstairs. She looked at Scout guiltily.

"I know you want to go for a walk every morning, but I'm just having trouble getting it together today. Sorry, boy. Maybe when Lisa comes home," she cringed for she knew it was inevitable; Lisa was coming back home. "She'll take you for nice long walks." She let Scout out where he did his business in the front yard under the trees, thus avoiding the rain. Beverly made a mental note of where he went and promised herself that she'd clean it up after work. It was raining after all.

She made herself a mocha, double chocolate, extra hot, and put it in her port-a-cup to take to work. She fixed a small bowl of corn flakes and as an afterthought sliced up and put in a slightly brown banana.

Gotta get rid of these bananas. They're pretty gross, she thought. Realizing that she didn't have the newspaper, she slipped on her shoes and ran out to grab the paper. She hadn't gotten too wet, just enough to make her hair a bit more frizzy and unmanageable. It sort of looked like it was trying to leave her head. The usual.

She sat down and ate her healthy breakfast, not really enjoying the flavor the mushy banana gave to her cereal. But she quickly paged through the newspaper, looking for information about the murder. Sure enough, there was an article on the second page. There was a picture of Joe. It wasn't very becoming, and she wondered where they got it. Maybe from his mother. He looked more like a convict than a victim. She closed the paper and folded it up, figuring she'd read the rest later.

"It's time for your breakfast, Scout. Your favorite time of the day."

She fed him, and as he happily crunched, Beverly went back upstairs to brush her teeth. She put on a pair of shoes that matched, grabbed her Columbia rain jacket, and went out to her car, forgetting her car keys. She went back in the house to get her keys. Feeling guilty leaving Scout for the day, she reached into the box of Milk Bones and gave one to Scout. He wagged his tail. She grabbed her keys and was out the side door and on her way to work.

Beverly noticed that her commute was even quicker leaving a little earlier, because traffic was really light. As she pulled up to the senior center, she saw the mob out front, many with walkers or canes. There must have been fifty people standing in the rain, waiting to get in. And it was only seven o'clock. She quickly parked and rummaged through her purse for her center keys. She thought she might as well fumble around in the comfort of her dry car, instead of in the rain.

She got the keys out and then rushed over to the front door, trying to avoid the rain. Her parking spot was way in the back of the lot since there were so many people. She scooted past the people like a halfback. A few of the people in line greeted her with a "Hello" and even more said, "What took you so long?" She wasn't accustomed to unlocking that door, so it took her a bit of jiggling before she got it right. Many of the seniors offered to help her, but she stubbornly refused. Finally, she got the door opened up. She let the people in, and they rushed to get out of the rain. Kat was one of the first seniors in. Beverly figured she didn't want to get her lovely silk dress ruined in the rain.

"Wait a minute. Let me get the lights on before you go walking around," Beverly said, going over to the bank of switches.

"It sure is cold in here," Ruth, the retired divorce attorney, said.

"Colder than a mother-in-law's smile, or even worse, an ex-mother-in-law's smile." Her friend Rod, who was a former bankruptcy attorney, countered.

"I'll turn the heat on in a minute, after I get the lights on," Beverly said as she began to flip switches.

"Let there be light!" one of the seniors said, and a few clapped. The seniors hurried into the main social room. The place was packed, and the gossip flew. They shook the rain off their coats and put them on the back of their chairs. Beverly retreated to the back of the building where the main heat controller was. She turned on the heat and heard the furnace kick in. Beverly walked around the building and made sure everything looked OK to start the day. She went down the hall where she had found Joe and stood by the place where his body had been. There was police tape around it and bloodstains on the floor. She cringed. She shook herself and then went over to the kitchen to start the coffee.

"No need to start the coffee, honey. I've already started it. There's decaf brewing too and some water is heating up for tea.

No worries." Beverly could have kissed Myrtle, one of her favorite volunteers. In a stage whisper she said, "Boy, I'm so sorry I missed all of the excitement yesterday. It would be my day off, huh!"

Beverly said, "It was eventful, all right."

"Are they going to get a new janitor soon?" she asked.

"I would think so, but you know how slowly the government works. Who knows how long it will take? There's lots of paperwork involved. Paul should know more. I'll talk with him when he gets in."

Myrtle said, "What do you want me to do to keep this crowd entertained? Of course, I don't think they need much entertainment today—they'll be talking about the murder all morning."

"I think you're right. Just make sure there's coffee at all times. By the way, is the regular ready? I can use a cup."

"Yes, I just heard it stop brewing." She put the pot on the counter.

"Can I pour you a cup, Myrtle?" Beverly asked.

"No thanks. I'll wait for the decaf. The regular really bothers my stomach. I guess my five-cup a day habit finally got the best of me," Myrtle said.

Beverly smiled to herself. She knew that Myrtle was at least eighty-five years old, and as active as ever. She certainly had no need for regular coffee; that was for sure. As Beverly poured herself a cup, a line formed behind her.

Myrtle inched over to Beverly and said, "I know this probably isn't the best timing, but I've been meaning to ask you if sometime I could play the piano here—you know—for the seniors. Oh, I know we've already got that nice young fellow. I wouldn't want to take his place. But maybe I could play once a week or so during lunchtime."

"I didn't know you played! Have you been playing long?" Beverly exclaimed.

"I started taking lessons two years ago, just after I finished my bachelor's degree."

Beverly's eyes got very large. "You earned your degree two years ago?"

"Well, actually two and a half years ago. I studied history. I think some of my classmates thought I lived through most of it—even the ancient history!"

"Myrtle, you amaze me."

Myrtle smiled.

"I never knew," Beverly continued. "That's wonderful. I would love for you to play piano any time you want. And maybe you could lead a history discussion sometime."

"I'd love to, on both counts, but I'll start with the piano. I'll work on my repertoire," Myrtle said.

Beverly moved over to the condiments area and put sugar and powdered cream into her cup and stirred it with a little, red, plastic coffee stirrer. She glanced over at the tables. The noise in the room was almost deafening, and more people were joining the existing group. She figured she would need to move some chairs from some of the classrooms over to the common area if people continued to come in. And she knew they would. So she unlocked the closest classroom and pulled out some chairs to bring over. Some of the seniors came to help her.

She went to the second closest classroom, unlocked the door, and started pulling out chairs from the table, but something prevented one of the chairs from moving. She thought perhaps that one of the teachers had left a parcel or something on the floor. She looked under the table to see what was causing the obstruction and saw a large pipe that looked like it was partially covered in dried blood. Stifling a scream, she quickly shooed out the seniors who were helping her and relocked the door.

She told her volunteer helpers, "Let's not use the chairs in this room. We're going to need this classroom for the Texas Hold 'em Poker game later today."

One of the men said, "No, we use the common room for that."

Thinking quickly, Beverly said, "You see how crowded the common room is today. I just figured we needed a backup plan." She unlocked the room across the hall and said, "Here, let's use these chairs."

Reluctantly, the volunteers complied.

Beverly said, "Would you please finish up here? I need to go to my office for a minute." They agreed, and she practically ran back to her little office. She rummaged through her purse and found Officer Swenson's card. She called his direct line and got him right away.

"Officer Swenson? This is Beverly Clavel, you know, from the senior center?"

"Yes, you sound excited. Are you OK? Is everything all right there?"

"I'm fine, everything's safe here. But I found a big pipe under one of the classroom tables. It looked like it was covered in blood. I was trying to move some chairs this morning, and I found it. I think I'm the only person who saw it. There were some seniors in the room moving chairs, but I shooed them out quickly."

"Lock up the classroom if you can. Don't touch anything. I'll be right over." He said.

"I did already—I mean lock the classroom. And no, I didn't touch anything."

She then called Paul's cell phone to tell him what she found. He said he was just turning the corner into the senior center parking lot.

"Oh my God," he said, "what next?"

Chapter Twelve

A short time later, Beverly spotted the two officers at the entrance to the main room. The chatter in the room ceased. She quickly walked up and whisked them into Paul's office. The chatter resumed as they walked out of the room.

When they got to Paul's office, Mike said, "Before we go into the classroom, let me know how you found the item."

Beverly answered, "As you saw, the center is packed today. We needed more chairs for the common area, so I thought I could move some chairs in from some of the classrooms. First I went to Room C—it's the closest one to the main room—and we moved some chairs. Some of the seniors helped me. Then I opened room D. When I tried to move one of the chairs, it got stuck. I was afraid that one of the teachers left something," she looked at him. "They do that often. Anyway, I looked under the table and saw that bar thing."

"Was anyone else with you? Did anyone else see it or touch it?" Jim asked.

"There were some seniors helping me move some chairs, but I shooed them out before they entered the room. So I don't believe anybody saw anything. And I didn't touch it. I made some excuse to not use those chairs, and I locked up the room."

Jim said, "Good. Let's take a look."

She led Paul and the police over to the classroom and put the key in the lock. The door slid open easily.

"Wait a minute!" Beverly exclaimed, "I'm almost positive that I locked the door. Now it's unlocked." They walked in and all peered under the table. There was nothing under the table.

Beverly exclaimed, "The pipe was right here! I saw it with my own eyes!"

"Are you sure it was this classroom? You have a lot of class-rooms here. Maybe there was a mix-up," Mike said.

She ran out to the classroom door. She saw the Classroom D plaque directly above the door. "I know it was here. Right next to Classroom C. This was the second room that I went in to get chairs."

"Why don't we just make sure?" She said and went to the other classrooms. One was stripped of its chairs. The other two were intact. None of them had a pipe under its table.

"I can't believe it!" she said. "I know I saw it. Somebody must have taken it."

Jim went over to the classroom window. It led out to the back of the building. He slipped on a pair of latex gloves from his back pocket and jiggled the locks.

"These locks aren't very sturdy, but there's no sign of forced entry. There aren't any screens on the windows, so it's hard to tell how someone got in."

Mike went over to take a look.

"I'm not crazy!" Beverly cried.

Paul said condescendingly, "Beverly, I know you've been through a lot these past two days. I can't even imagine what it must have been like for you yesterday. Maybe you were just imagining it. Stress does funny things to people."

"Like you should know," Beverly said under her breath. Out loud, she said, "I wasn't imagining it; I know I saw that bar!"

Jim said, "Mike, I'd like to call in the crime scene investigators again. Even though the pipe is gone, they may be able to find something. This room was thoroughly searched yesterday so the pipe, if it really was here, must have been planted after the CSI team left yesterday."

"OK," Jim said and stepped out the door of the classroom.

Paul said, "This is going to be very disruptive to our seniors, Beverly, would you try to distract them or something? Maybe play a game of bingo? You know what to do."

She fumed as she made her way to the common area.

I hate it when people patronize me, especially Paul. The nerve of that guy, she thought. When she got to the common area, she decided that rather than trying to distract or lie, that she would just make an announcement to the seniors. She knew they'd find everything out anyway. Looking at the many anxious faces, she went over by the coffee counter.

"May I have your attention please?" she said very loudly. The chatter almost stopped. Beverly saw that even Ruth and Tilly quieted down.

"Attention, please!" said Tilly, very loudly.

"What's she saying?" a few people said "Shhhh! She's trying to say something."

"Ladies and gentlemen, I'm sure you know that our custodian was murdered yesterday. Some of you were here. The police are still investigating. A small group of investigators is coming back this morning. I want you all to please stay in this common area while they work. If anyone bothers them, we may need to close down the center for the day. So your cooperation is most appreciated."

There were murmurs of approval, and Beverly went back to Paul and the officers.

When she peeked into Paul's office, she saw sympathetic looks directed at her. She felt furious.

"I'll be in my office." she said and stormed down the hall.

Maybe I am imagining things, she thought, logging on to her computer for the day. But I can't be. I have to believe my own eyes. I couldn't move that chair. And there was a pipe with blood on it. I saw it!

She checked her calendar. She was facilitating a group later in the week—in Room D ironically. It was a discussion about strokes. A retired nurse was going to speak about the warning signs of a stroke. *Maybe I'm having a stroke, she thought. I wish I knew the warning signs now!*

Her phone rang. Her caller ID said it was her ex, Herb. "Oh joy!"

"Herb," Beverly spoke into the phone in a highly agitated voice.

"What have you done to Lisa?" he said.

"What do you mean?" she asked, trying her best to stay calm and civil.

"She called me last night. She said she's dropping out of school."

"I just found out about it yesterday too. I knew nothing about it. Did you know she was flunking out?" she asked.

"No, I've gotten no notice."

"You'd think since we're paying the bills we'd know."

"I'm paying the bills, not you. And apparently we wouldn't know. I called the school this morning, and they said they're not authorized to send notices and grades to anyone but the student—privacy and all that. Can you believe that? Idiots!" Herb exclaimed.

Beverly said nothing as she was too taken aback and stunned by his "paying the bills comment." How did she ever love this man?

"Doesn't matter. I guess they consider the students adults. Its crap, and I can't believe it. She should never have gone to that liberal school," he said.

"I wish she wasn't, but she said she's dropping out and that she'll be home in a few days. I'm not happy about it either."

"Well, it seems like you probably talked her into it. Like mother, like daughter. She's going to make the same stupid mistake you did."

"Ok, that's it, you JERK!" she said. "The only mistake I made was marrying YOU!" Beverly slammed down the phone so hard she was sure it would crack.

Chapter Thirteen

Beverly noticed that the seniors tried really hard to stay in the common area, but they couldn't bear not knowing what was going on, if for no other reason than being "in the know" before their friends. Beverly saw that they casually sent out scouts. They pretended to go down the hall to the restroom but really were checking out what was going on. Beverly noticed that, as usual, Tilly was the ringleader. She knew that she assigned different people to different tasks like the most highly skilled military strategist. Beverly figured that it was driving her crazy not knowing what the police were looking at in the classroom.

Beverly made her way over to Tilly's table. As she walked past, she noticed that none of the people at the table, or anywhere nearby, would meet her eye. She went to the coffee pot and poured herself a cup. One of the volunteers, Sally, was refreshing the condiments.

Beverly said, "Sally, Tilly is up to something. She and her posse look very guilty!"

"Oh, I don't think so," Sally said, looking away. "Say, are they still having the dance tonight? That will take everyone's mind off of everything."

Beverly slapped her head. "Oh, I almost forgot about the dance! After getting up and opening so early I'm just not running on all cylinders. I need to double-check with the band and make sure they're still planning to come. They probably heard all about the murder and don't know if the dance is still on. Thanks for reminding me, Sally. And I need to make sure I go home before the dance to feed and let out Scout."

Sally said, "Oh, I want to meet Scout. He sounds a lot like my dog Max." Beverly knew that Sally's black lab of many years had died not too long ago. "I still miss him. You should bring Scout in sometime. I bet the seniors would just adore him. He is good with people isn't he?"

"Oh yes, he hasn't met a potential handout that he doesn't like," Beverly said, smiling.

"You should check with Paul. I bet it would be OK with him. Unless he's one of those misguided cat people," she said, looking heavenward.

Beverly chuckled, "Good idea, maybe I will ask him." She walked back to her office, thoughtful.

Her telephone message light was blinking so she checked her messages. She had a message from Rosie, the band leader, reconfirming the gig. She also had a message from the police officer Jim Swenson, informing her that the crime scene area where the body was found could be cleaned up. He gave her the name of two companies that specialize in that type of cleanup. She jotted them down.

First she called Rosie. She answered on the fifth ring. Beverly was used to waiting. Whenever she needed to call some of the seniors, she gave them plenty of time to answer the phone.

"Rosie! I'm so glad you called. Yes, we're still on for the five thirty to eight thirty dance. Is everything OK on your end?"

"Absolutely. The boys and I are looking forward to it. We always love playing at the center. I heard about the murder. Is everything all right? Who was killed?"

"It was Joe, our custodian. It was horrible. But don't worry; just after we finish our conversation, I'm going to call a company that cleans everything up. No problem."

"That would be a hell of a job, cleaning up crime scenes! We can always postpone. That would be no problem."

"Oh no, Rosie, everyone looks forward to your dances. They'd be so disappointed if we called it off. And I think it will be a great distraction for them. Maybe take their minds off of what happened."

"OK then, we'll be there at about four thirty to set up. Is it going to be in the same area as last time?"

"Yes," Beverly said, writing herself a reminder to move some of the chairs to the sides of the room to leave room for a dance floor. "I'm looking forward to seeing you then."

Then, Beverly dialed the clean up companies. The first company on the list couldn't come out until the next day, so she called the second one on the list. She explained the "mess" and they said they'd be right out. Beverly walked over to Paul's office and informed him of the situation. Paul's face was burning.

"Those police officers called my Wes last night. They want to question him, do you believe it? What would he have to do with anything?"

"They want to question Wes? Why?"

"They didn't really say. They just said something about him maybe putting some light on the investigation." Paul looked stricken. "Do you think they suspect *me* of killing Joe or do you think they suspect Wes? It seems crazy!"

"Why would they even think that?"

"Well, it must be because I told them that Joe and I didn't really get along and that I had written him up and put him on probation for ethnic slurs when he insulted Laura. Sure, he wasn't my best friend but I wouldn't kill him."

"Of course you didn't. Had he ever shown any animosity toward you because you're gay?"

"Naturally. He's a big bully, or I guess he *was* a big bully. He knew he was walking a fine line because I was his boss. But he felt like he was protected since he'd been with the center so much longer than me. I think he got the job because he was friends with somebody. But it's hard for me to believe that he had any friends. More likely he had some dirt on somebody." Paul was starting to calm down.

"But I don't understand why he should care so much about the job. I mean, I can't imagine it was that great a job, though. I mean, working as a janitor in a senior center?" Beverly said.

"Are you kidding? He was paid pretty well, and he could be as ornery as he wanted to be. He basically worked reasonable hours, took smoke breaks whenever he wanted, and did as little work as possible," he said.

"But you put him on probation. That must have really ticked him off."

"The incident with Laura was just one of many. It usually takes a lot to put somebody on probation. And then it takes a lot to get the person that's on probation fired."

"Really? I didn't know that."

"According to *Policies and Procedures* I'm not supposed discuss his personal case, except on a need to know basis." Beverly knew that Paul was nothing if not a "play by the book" kind of bureaucrat. "But I guess I can discuss a little. After all, he is dead."

"But getting back to the fact that they want to talk to Wes. Why would they want to talk with Wes?" she asked again.

"Well," he said, as Beverly thought, *Now we're getting somewhere.*

"I've been getting threatening phone calls."

"No! Here? At the center?"

"No, at home," he said.

"What kind of phone calls? And when did they start?"

"They started several months ago. Maybe twice a week I would get a phone call calling me a faggot and worse. You know, I'm kind of used to it. I mean, you can't have gotten through high school acting the least bit gay without being called all kinds of names."

Beverly remembered Lisa's friend Matthew who was openly gay and all of the criticism and teasing that he endured going through high school and even later. "That must have been hard."

"Goes with the territory," he dismissed it with a wave of his hand. "Anyway, these phone calls were coming in. I started tracking the caller ID and called the phone company. They were from various pay phones around town. So there was really nothing I could do. But Wes was furious. He's a bit of a hot-tempered guy and doesn't take a lot of shit. Maybe I said something to the police that made them want to talk with him. Who knows? I really wish Wes was openly gay. He acts like it's such a big secret."

"Why doesn't he just come out? I mean, it's not like it's any big deal." Beverly said.

"Easier said than done, my friend. Only our closest friends know. Wes says that it would break his mom and dad's hearts if they knew."

"Really? I didn't know that kind of thing still happened."

"You'd be surprised," Paul sighed.

"But back to the phone calls," Beverly tilted her head. "It still seems odd. Why now?" she said.

"Like maybe they're thinking that Wes killed somebody to preserve my honor or something. It's so, so, Jane Austen!"

"Actually, it seems kind of romantic," Beverly said. That put a smile on Paul's face. "Oh, by the way, everything's set for the dance tonight. Rosie and the Boys will be here at four thirty to set up. I'll collect the money."

"It's $3.50, right?" Paul said, scratching his head.

"Yes, we had to raise it from $3.25. I'm sure some of the seniors will have something to say about that! But that covers the cost of the band and snacks. I hope there's a good turnout. Especially some men. There's always a shortage. And I hope Nathan Small comes again. He was quite the hit with the ladies at the last dance."

"Nathan Small? I don't remember him," Paul remarked.

"He just started coming to the center maybe once a week. He has come to a couple of the dances, and he's quite the ladies man. He's a fabulous dancer."

"That's great. I'm sure he's a real charmer. And maybe the ladies will turn their attention to him, instead of trying to fix me up with their granddaughters." They both laughed.

"Oh," Beverly said, slapping her forehead, "I need to stop at the store and pick up the snacks. And by the way, one of the volunteers suggested that I bring my dog Scout to the center once in a while, you know, to interact with the seniors. That might be fun."

"Well, I don't know, it might go against the *Policies and Procedures*. I'd have to check. But I think it would be OK."

"I'll just bring him in on a trial basis. I wouldn't dream of letting him come during a lunch hour. He's the biggest beggar in the world. Oh, I better get out to the front. The cleanup crew should be here any minute to clean up the murder scene. In fact, they might already be there waiting for me."

"And the CSI team is done in room D also, so be sure to have the cleanup crew take a look at the floor in there too, just in case." Paul's phone rang, and Beverly waved goodbye and stepped out of his office and closed his door.

She walked over to the front of the building and waited for the hazardous materials cleaners. And she thought she had a crummy job.

Chapter Fourteen

Beverly zoomed over to the grocery store to pick up the snacks. Even though the parking lot was nearly empty, she pulled in a little bit away from the entrance, so as not to get her car dinged. She ran inside, got the snacks, and then rushed back to her car. While she was putting her bags into the trunk, her shopping cart started rolling away in the wind. She dropped her last bag into the trunk and ran over to grab the cart. It has mysteriously stopped, as if something was blocking it.

She stopped short when she saw the body of a woman lying in the parking lot. She was very still and looked like she was leaking blood. Beverly screamed and pulled her phone out of her purse and dialed 911. She told the dispatcher the situation. Shortly thereafter, she heard sirens, and she slumped onto the blacktop of the parking lot.

First a fire truck came, and she flagged the firemen over to the body. They emerged from the truck quickly to work on the woman. That was when Beverly took a close look at the woman's head. She had dark black hair, but only on half of her head, just like Joe Boulden's friend! She inched closer and saw that it was probably her. She couldn't believe it.

Then she saw a police car careening in. She saw her two new friends, Jim and Mike, run up. By the time they arrived, an ambulance was pulling up. Two EMTs went to work on the woman. Beverly listened in.

"What's the status?" Jim asked the EMT, who was administering CPR.

"She's lost a lot of blood. She took a bullet in her head. She doesn't have a pulse. I'm not sure how long she's been lying here.

That lady over there found her. She was way in the back of the parking lot."

Beverly noted that she looked like she'd been hit from behind. She surmised that she'd been dragged to that spot, maybe hidden. Her head was covered in blood.

Beverly realized that Jim and Mike still hadn't noticed her standing there.

Then Jim gasped and said, "Oh my god!" What are you doing here?"

Beverly looked straight in their eyes and said, "I found the body. With my shopping cart!"

Beverly continued to watch as the drama unfolded. She saw that the EMT stopped administering CPR. The ambulance crew brought over the stretcher. They strapped the woman in and put her in the ambulance to take her to the hospital. By then quite a crowd had gathered.

Mike's booming voice said, "Back up, folks. The show's over. Please let us do our work."

I'm sure not leaving, Beverly thought.

Beverly saw Jim pull out his cell phone, and she listened while he called the CSI team. Then Jim pulled some police tape out of the squad car and cordoned off the area between the two cars.

Beverly heard Jim say "Did she have any ID on her?" as he and Mike put on their latex gloves.

"I have her purse here," Mike said. Beverly noted that it was a very large patchwork type purse, blue and green mostly. He fumbled around and found her wallet.

"Of course we'll have to get a positive ID, but her driver's license says she's Bethany Ann Jones. She's twenty-seven years old. Looks like she lives not far from here." Rummaging through her purse, he pulled out a sheet of paper. "And she's going on a trip this weekend," he said, reading the sheet. "It's an e-ticket for her and Joe Boulden to Washington D.C. Leaving Friday at three thirty, returning Sunday night."

Beverly walked in between the two men. "That was Joe's friend, wasn't it? I noticed her hair right away. Tickets in her purse?"

Jim said, "Tickets to Washington, D.C.?"

Beverly said, "I think it's unlikely that she killed Joe, since they were planning a trip together. What else is in her purse? That's a gigantic purse."

Mike rummaged some more when he came upon an envelope. It was unsealed, so he looked inside.

"Two tickets to the Holocaust Museum. Sunday at twelve thirty."

Beverly said, "That museum is so popular that you need to get advance tickets. You can get them online. You can do that with a few of the monuments. They're free." She looked at the men, one at a time. "I just took a trip to Washington, D.C.., a couple years ago. I for one don't think that they were just planning an innocent trip to the museum. We need to find out what they were up to."

Mike said, "Beverly, I think we can manage without your help. In fact, we need to take your statement. Then shouldn't you get back to work?"

She said, "Anything incriminating in that big purse?"

"Doesn't look like it. But that doesn't mean she didn't have something in her home."

Beverly said, "I've got to get back to work."

They quickly took Beverly's statement, and she went to her car. Opening the car door she said, "Two bodies in two days. What next?"

Chapter Fifteen

After the harrowing trip to the grocery store, Beverly went home to feed Scout and let him out, then returned to the senior center to help set up for the dance. She didn't see any of the seniors around, so she decided that most had gone home to change. She smiled as she thought that many of them got very dressed up for the dance. Dances always proved to be popular events and were usually well attended, even by the people who were not really ambulatory. She went into the main room of the center and moved some of the tables and chairs out toward the sides of the room with help from some of the volunteers. There was plenty of space in the middle for dancing. The coffee counter was filled with the snacks and soda pop that Beverly had purchased.

The band arrived promptly at four thirty, and Beverly helped them set up. Once they were ready they began to warm up. Beverly could hear the songs. There was electricity in the air. People started showing up at five fifteen, fifteen minutes before the dance was to start, so Beverly quickly set up the check-in table and got out the cash box. Paul arrived and took over the cash box. He was dressed nicely, as usual. Beverly went into the room to supervise.

Beverly sat down at one of the far tables. She saw that Tilly and her gang showed up first, and took a table close to the band. The band got started at about 5:25 with a fast fifties number. Beverly smiled, because it lent a very festive tone to the start of the dance. She was hoping that lots of men would show up. She knew that demographically Portland was similar every other city in the country: as the population aged, there were many more women than men. This statistic was borne out at the senior center, where there were probably three women for every one man. So the men who came to dance were always extremely busy, even the ones who claimed to "not know how to dance." They always had many willing teachers.

Beverly noticed some murmuring at Tilly's table and saw the source of their whispers. Nathan Small was coming in. He was by far the best dancer at the center. He barely found a place to sit down when Tilly rushed over to him and asked him to dance. It was a waltz. He stood up with good cheer and took Tilly's elbow. They were the first dancers on the floor.

Beverly was sorry that the seniors didn't have the same lack of inhibitions that her daughter's generation did, where everyone got up to dance, even without partners. In fact, Lisa said that it was often more fun to dance with her girlfriends than going to a dance with a date and being stuck with him all evening. No, the seniors were definitely of a different generation.

Beverly smiled as she watched Nathan and Tilly glide along the dance floor. Nathan was dressed in a beautiful navy-blue suit with a crisp white shirt and maroon tie. Tilly was wearing a loose turquoise dress with matching shoes. It looked as if she had just had her short, curly hair done; there was not a tress out of place. She was much smaller than Nathan, but that didn't matter while dancing. She was looking up into his face and smiling. Oh yes, that Nathan was a smooth operator!

When the waltz music stopped, Tilly reluctantly went back to her seat and so did Nathan. There was another man at his table named Bill. Beverly couldn't remember his last name. Beverly knew he was notorious from a few years back when, after he had lost his driver's license, he saved up his Social Security money that was intended to be used for rent and instead bought a second-hand car. He got himself a little green beret and drove around town for a couple months without a license. Since he lived in an apartment, he was able to park his car without anyone really knowing it was his.

He was a happy driver until his daughter found out that he'd taken his rent money and bought the car. She promptly had a fit and sold the car. He still complained about what his daughter did with the car and also his freedom. Bill had been coming to the senior center for years; he was a widower who had lost his wife about ten years ago. Despite the fact that he was a single man of a certain age, he resisted getting seriously involved with anyone, even though all the women tried. A friendly man, he took to Nathan right away when Nathan started coming to the center a few months back, despite the fact that Nathan was rather quiet and reserved.

The band played a faster number, and Bill got up and asked a woman at the next table to dance. She giggled and let herself be led to the dance floor. Beverly was happy to see that a few more men had shown up. There were several couples on the dance floor, and it was only six o'clock. The dance was proving to be a success, so Beverly decided to talk with Paul, who was still sitting at the check-in table. She sat down on the chair next to him.

"Looks like there's more people here today than at any previous dance," Beverly said.

Paul replied, "It's probably because of the murder. I guess that's one good thing to come out of it."

"The seniors seem to like Rosie and the Boys. We'll have to have them again."

"I agree. And hardly anybody complained about the twenty-five cent increase. Just one person, who shall remain nameless," he made a sour-puss face, imitating one of the senior men to a tee.

Beverly laughed, "You look just like him. By the way, did the police talk with Wes?" Beverly said, changing the subject.

"They did. They called him at work to talk with him; he was working really late last night. Seemed like that was rude, but I guess that's what Wes asked them to do—you know, call him at work. They asked him where he was at the time of the murder. I couldn't believe it. Can you imagine. That's a real stretch if they think Wes would have killed him."

"That does seem pretty unlikely. They must be really desperate for suspects if they talked with Wes," she said.

"That's for sure. Well, at least he had an alibi. He was working at the time, and his assistant was with him."

"That's good. Hopefully they'll leave him alone. Had Wes even met Joe?" she asked.

"Yes. What a disaster. It was just a chance meeting at the hardware store of all places. Joe nailed our relationship right away, even though Wes tried to keep it a secret. And Joe was pretty obnoxious with him. I remember him asking Wes whether he was the husband or the wife in our relationship. The nerve of that guy."

"Unbelievable. When I was talking with Lisa about the murder, she said that Joe made a pass at her when she was here one day. And she was only about sixteen or seventeen at the time. He had to be at least ten years older than her. I hadn't known about that. It really made me mad. Good thing I didn't know about it then, I probably would have killed him myself. Oh—I didn't mean to say that," she said.

Just then, two ladies walked up to get in to the dance. They were very dressed up. One had an apricot-colored dress and her friend was wearing a pale-green dress that was a bit too tight at the bust line. They both had very uncomfortable looking heels with matching purses.

Paul took their money, "Don't you two look lovely! Have fun ladies!"

They said, "If we can't be good we'll be careful!"

"Words to live by," Paul said. After they walked in, he said, "I think they may have had a few cocktails before coming tonight, I just hope they didn't drive."

"Maybe Bill can drive them home." they both laughed at that.

"Can you handle the dance, Paul? I'd like to finish up some paperwork in my office if that's OK."

"Sure, no problem. I'll probably move this table out of the way in a little bit. I'm sure most everybody that's coming is here already. I'll go in."

"Are you going to dance with some of the ladies?" Beverly said hopefully. "You know it would make their night."

"Of course. It's the best part of my job. There are some really good dancers out there. They are so much fun. As long as they don't go on and on about their granddaughters all night. Oh, if only I were straight." they laughed.

Beverly walked back to her office. Walking through the hallway, she saw no evidence of the week's events; everything had been cleaned up by the cleaning crew. The hallway had a faintly antiseptic smell to it.

She decided to look more closely at Joe's work areas since the police hadn't been there yet. A quick look in the supply cabinet told her that nothing was amiss there. Then she opened up the other small working area, she pulled the light cord at the top of the closet. It was just a bare bulb at the top of the closet. The closet had a musty odor. There was a green jacket hung up on a little hook to the side. There was a small desk tucked into the closet with papers stacked on top of it. Beverly stepped aside and peeked at the pile.

She started looking at the papers. At the very top of the pile was information that looked like it was pulled from the web. The pages included instructions on how to mix various gases to create toxic fumes. Below that was a pile of instructions on making homemade bombs using common household items. Below that were some more instructions on more gas mixtures. Beverly felt ill as she thumbed through the pile of papers, finding more and more bomb recipes, gas recipes and such.

What a lunatic! She thought. *He really must have been planning on gassing or bombing the Holocaust Museum this weekend. I wonder if the murderer knew of the plan and was stopping him.*

She locked the closet again and went to her office to call the police officers.

"You're not going to believe what I just found," Beverly said, just after Jim answered.

Chapter Sixteen

"Remember you found tickets to Washington D.C. in the dead girl's purse?" Beverly asked Jim on the phone, "I probably would have known if Joe was taking time off of work, but since he was taking the trip over the weekend I wouldn't have been aware of it. And probably neither would Paul. Do you think the girl was a Nazi sympathizer or a neo-Nazi or something? Were they part of some group? They must have been planning something," she said.

"I need to check into her background some more. Her name was Bethany Ann Jones. Her mother calls her Beth or Bethy. She seemed clean, but she had a brother with a rap sheet a mile long," he said.

Beverly said, "If they were part of some type of hate group, then they probably had a number of enemies. I'd like to check to see if anything special was scheduled for the Holocaust Museum this weekend. Joe and Beth may have just been planning some type of protest or something. Who knows? I can ask around at the senior center to see about any animosity between some of the seniors and the custodian. I don't know how deep it went. Maybe I can poke around a little and see who may know something. Anything may help. There's a dance going on now. I'll go over there and mingle a little."

"Feel free to call me with any information. I'll call tomorrow to set up some time to go through his things. And thanks, Beverly," Jim said.

"You're welcome. I'll see if I can find anything out. Bye," she said and hung up.

She sat quietly for a moment.

Wow, another person dead, she thought. *Even if she was a hateful person, and I don't really know that, there's another family grieving.* She forced herself to stand up and she went back through the mildly antiseptic smelling hallway and over to the social room where the band had switched to another number. Many of the seniors were up doing the jitterbug, including Paul. It looked like the dance was a success. The band was very versatile. Even the folks who didn't care to dance looked like they were having fun. Some had taken out decks of cards and were munching snacks and playing various card games. Beverly's former attorney friends Ruth and Rod were at one of the tables, along with Laura Goldstein and a woman that Beverly had not met.

Ruth called her over, "Beverly! How are you? I'd like you to meet my neighbor, Viola Schultz." Viola held out her hand and gave Beverly a surprisingly firm grip. Beverly always hesitated when shaking hands with any of the seniors, since many had painful arthritis in their hands.

Beverly said, "Viola—I've always loved that name. I'm pleased to meet you. Are you having a good time?"

"Oh yes, this is just a ball. Now, I'm not much of a dancer, but I do love to play cards. And I've met so many nice people."

"Is this your first visit to the center?" Beverly asked. "I don't remember seeing you here before."

"Yes, it is. And what a wonderful place." she exclaimed.

"Well I hope it's the first visit of many."

Rod pulled up a chair. "Why don't you sit in on a round of cards? We're playing Texas Hold'em poker."

"Sure, why not? But I'm surprised you're able to get out of dancing, Rod. Usually men are pretty scarce around these parts," Beverly said.

"Since I've stepped on so many toes, even the most determined dancers have stopped asking me," he said.

Ruth said, looking at Beverly, "Don't believe him for a minute. I think he's just being lazy." she said, dealing each player two cards face down and then discarding the bum card.

Laura said, "Ever since Nathan Small showed up and started coming to the dances, I think all the other men feel intimidated."

Viola was watching Small and practically swooning, "Oh, isn't he just the best dancer?" she said.

"He sure is! Not many men can dance as well as he can," Laura said.

"Have you known him very long, Laura?" Beverly asked, "I mean did you know him before he started coming to the center? I thought you mentioned that you had."

"We attend the same synagogue. You know, there aren't that many synagogues in Portland. The one that we attend is quite large," she said.

"Is that the one in Northwest?" Beverly knew that Portlanders often referred to parts of town by Northwest, Southwest, Southeast, and Northeast, then of course downtown and various named neighborhoods, like the Pearl District. The Northwest section generally comprised many stately older buildings and some newly refurbished condos. It had many upscale shops and restaurants.

"Yes. It pulls people in from all over Portland."

"I see."

"Come to think of it, he and I were on a committee together last year. Right about this time of year. Our synagogue sponsored Yom HaShoah."

"What's that?" Viola asked.

"It's the Day of Remembrance. Every year for about ten years, Portland and many other cities have honored the victims of the Holocaust on the Day of Remembrance. On that day, we say the names of a small list of people who were killed in the Holocaust. It's much more meaningful to attach the names of actual human beings to the numbers. It's just hard for people to grasp the fact that over six-million Jews were killed. It's in unfathomable number," she said.

"I agree. It's overwhelming. What a tradition. This is the first I've heard of it. Thank you for telling me about it," Beverly said. They were silent for moment.

"OK, now let's start the betting," Rod said, lifting the mood.

Ruth said, "You always get a lucky hand, Rod. Mine are always pathetic."

"Must be clean livin' Ruth. I don't have all those divorcees on my conscience," he replied. "Speaking of which, Beverly, has any progress been made with your ex?"

"Nothing since he tried to get me to mediation. As you and Ruth suggested, I'm not going into mediation until I speak with an attorney."

Ruth said, "That's smart. I'm sure Herb, that's Beverly's ex," she said, looking at Viola, "will smile and simper, and say that he wants to protect your joint assets. But believe me—he has his own interests in mind. You need to protect yourself."

Viola added, "My daughter got a divorce two years ago. She was out of the workforce for ten years, caring for her two children. It was really hard for her to get a job that paid decently, even though she worked for many years before having children."

Ruth said, "That happens a lot. In fact, I just read an article in the paper discussing a study of how the financial circumstances of women change when they take off time from the workforce to care for children. Their finances are very much compromised."

"It just doesn't seem right. She probably worked harder raising those kids than she did when she was paid to work," Beverly exclaimed.

"Honey," Laura said, "you're preaching to the choir. I raised four boys, and it was work, twenty-four/seven. You never get a break!"

"Well the good news, if there is any, is that my daughter's ex-husband has to pay for her to go back to school. She's getting her master's degree now. He's paying all of the child care costs while she completes her degree. So, hopefully, she'll be in a much better position with her degree and her previous experience," Viola said.

Rod added, "Maybe you can go back to school Beverly, if you want to. I can't imagine that this job pays near enough to live on. I mean no offense or anything."

"All I can say is that I'm glad we're not betting real money here!" Beverly said with a laugh.

As they finished their round of poker, Beverly's cell phone rang.

"Excuse me, I better take this." She said, getting up and quickly walking out to the hall where it was quieter.

"Mom!" It was Lisa.

"Hi honey. How are you?"

"Mom, I haven't been straight with you. I'm pregnant."

"You're WHAT?" Beverly shrieked to her daughter on the other end of the phone.

"I'm pregnant Mom. That's the real reason I'm dropping out," Lisa said, somewhat calmly.

"I didn't even know you were dating anyone! Was it one of those 'hook ups' that I've been reading about in the paper? Do you know who the father is?"

"Oh Mom, you're so dramatic. Of course I know who the father is. But the problem is that he's married. He's one of my professors."

"Oh my god! One of your professors!"

"It's not like he's an old man or anything. He's maybe in his early forties."

"And his wife just didn't understand him ..."

"Don't make fun of me, Mom. I know it was a big mistake."

"And he's not leaving his wife and kids."

"No, he's not. I was a fool, but I'm going to make the best of it. I'm coming home. I'm having the baby."

"How far along are you?" she asked.

"I'm just about two months along."

"Can't you finish up your semester? At least get that behind you?"

"I'm really flunking out, Mom. I'm sorry. I've been really unfocused this semester. You see, John and I broke up, then got back together, and then broke up again. It's been really, really bad."

Beverly felt for her daughter. And she knew that Herb would kill the professor when he found out.

"Have you told Dad?" she asked.

"No, I was hoping you would," Lisa said, her voice practically a whisper.

"Not a chance! I know he's your father and I know you love him, but I haven't been able to have a civil conversation with him since he left. I'm sorry, but this one's yours," Beverly said.

"Yes, you're right. I'm sorry Mom, I'll call him right away. I love you."

"I love you too, dear," she closed the phone carefully.

She put her head in her hands. She wondered how long it would take Herb to call her and try to blame this event on her. She put her cell phone on mute.

Chapter Seventeen

L ater that evening, Beverly answered Jim's phone call at her desk. She mentioned what Laura Goldstein had said to her about the Day of Remembrance and that she thought that the day was coming up soon this year.

Jim said, "Since we were working on other angles, I haven't been able to search Joe's work area. I'd like to do that now. Can I come over now? I'd like to see what you uncovered. Did he have an office?"

"No, not really. He kept the supply cabinet organized and kept track of the supplies and told me when I needed to order things. He had a small student-type desk in another small closet. That's what I told you about—you know, where I found that paperwork. He wasn't in there very often. I think I mentioned before that he was a smoker and used to go out to his truck on his breaks to have a smoke. But, anyway, I'd be happy to unlock those areas so you can take a look."

"That would be great. I should be there in about fifteen minutes or so if that's convenient for you."

"That's fine. And a word of warning—be sure you sneak past the common area. Don't let any of the ladies see you or they'll want to dance with you."

"That's what my partner Mike said. I didn't believe him," Jim said.

"Believe him. I'll see you soon."

No sooner had she hung up when she noticed that someone had left a message on her cell phone. Since she had muted it, it hadn't rung, but it was vibrating. She opened it up and checked her messages. She was not surprised when she heard Herb's voice,

"What are we going to do about Lisa? I can't believe it! Where are you?" and he hung up.

She had a delicious thought. Instead of having Lisa come home to her, she could have Lisa go to live with Herb and his girlfriend. Beverly was certain that the young girlfriend had much more energy than she did. Yes, that's what she could propose. Beverly would sell the house and move to a nice two-bedroom condo downtown. Then Herb, his girlfriend, Lisa, and the baby could live all as one big happy family. Herb's girlfriend will no doubt get pregnant soon, and then the two babies could grow up together. She sat musing until Jim walked in.

"Penny for your thoughts?" he said.

"Believe me, you don't want to know. Let me get the keys. I'll show you the two areas." She unlocked one of her drawers and pulled out a large set of keys. She stood up and stretched. "What a long day. It was smart of you to sneak past the dance. Did it look like most of the people were having fun?"

"Oh, yes. Those people were really moving. A fair number were sitting down, drinking punch and playing cards, but there were probably about five or six couples on the dance floor. Everyone seemed to be having a good time."

"I'm glad. When I first started working here, they didn't have any dances. Now, they're our most popular event. We try to have a dance at least twice a month. It's a great way for people to get to know each other." She led him to the supply cabinet and unlocked the door. She pulled the light cord, and it lit a bare light bulb lighting up the small cabinet. The supply cabinet was very neat and tidy but had a bit of a chemical smell.

Beverly pointed to the three shelves on the left side. "All of the cleaning supplies are on this side. There are more cleaning supplies in the kitchen, but generally the volunteers take care of the kitchen cleaning, not Joe. Except the kitchen floors, Joe did those."

Beverly pointed to the bottles of industrial-strength chemicals that were used for different purposes. In the middle of the small room was a large bucket with some water and what smelled like floor cleaner inside. There was a large mop sticking out and the bucket had a wringer on the side.

"And over on this side," she said, pointing to the right, "are the paper products."

There were stacks of wrapped toilet paper, paper towel rolls, and folded-up paper towels to be used in the bathrooms.

"What are these keys for?" Jim asked, pointing to sets of keys arranged on hooks.

"Oh, those are keys to all of the rooms in the building. You know, the classrooms, my office, Paul's office, and the kitchen area—and the keys to the toilet-paper dispensers and towel dispensers."

"You have to lock them up?" He asked.

"You'd be surprised how often toilet paper and paper towels get stolen from public buildings. Most of the time it's just kids that sneak in wanting to get toilet paper to TP someone's house."

"I believe that. Does everything look in order here? Is anything missing?"

"Everything looks copasetic here. I know because I've had to fill in for Joe from time to time. Let's look at the other closet." She locked the supply closet door and walked in front of Jim.

"Is the supply closet normally locked?" He asked.

"No, generally during the day, Joe would open this supply cabinet and keep it open all day. That was so that anybody could get supplies freely without having to bother him. The kitchen workers especially were always getting more paper towels and such. I hadn't really thought about it, but that meant that all of the keys, except the front-door keys were available pretty much all day to anyone."

"Yes, that does pose a problem. Was it just you, Paul, and the volunteers who knew about this supply cabinet? How many volunteers do you have here?"

"We have about ten volunteers. Most of them only work a few hours a week if that. And they all knew of the supply closet. But I'm sure they've asked others, people who weren't volunteers, to fetch things from the supply cabinet from time to time."

"So it probably wasn't a secret that the keys were in here."

"Yes, you're right." She said and walked in front of him. Beverly let Jim to the other closet, Joe's workspace. "The other closet is over here. This one, as far as I know, was always kept locked," she said, and unlocked the door. "This is where I found the bomb-making paperwork," she said as she opened the door. "Shocking, isn't it? I truly had no idea."

Jim slipped on his gloves and went through the paperwork. "It's shocking all right." He said.

"Do you think he was planning a disturbance at the Holocaust Museum this weekend?"

"No way to prove it, but it wouldn't surprise me," He said. "Can I have a box? I'd like to take these papers back to the station."

"Sure thing," she said, and then went to the supply cabinet to get a box. After she got back, Jim packed up the papers. Beverly led him out of the building. She headed back to the dance thinking about who would want to kill Joe and his girlfriend.

Chapter Eighteen

After a long evening, Beverly and Paul straightened up, locked all of the rooms in the senior center, and then locked the front door. The seniors and the band were long gone. Paul said, "Do you want to go get a drink? Wes is planning to meet me down the street."

"I think I'll pass. I just want to get home and take a nice, hot bath. But give Wes my best, and I'll see you tomorrow."

"OK. I'll open up early, so why don't you come in late, like about ten o'clock, OK?"

"That would be great, Paul. I think I need a nice sleep-in. I'm glad the dance went so well."

"Me too. Thanks for all of your hard work. Until tomorrow!" he gave her a big hug.

Beverly went to her car and drove home on autopilot. As she was pulling up in the driveway, her phone rang. "Hello," she grumbled.

"Hi, it's Laurie. I'm coming over and we're going to have a girl's night."

"No, not tonight. I'm dead on my feet. You would not *believe* what happened today," Beverly said.

"Sorry. I'm only three blocks away. I'm picking you up and we're going to go pick out some hair color. You haven't been keeping up with your roots, have you?" Laurie was nothing if not a consummate hair fanatic.

"You've got to be kidding."

"Oh, never mind, I know what color you need. I'll just pick something up on the way. Don't worry. I'll do all the work. You don't have to do a thing," Laurie argued.

"OK, fine," Beverly said reluctantly, and hung up. She pulled into her driveway and garage. She could hear Scout's excited barking and cries. She opened the door, and Scout flew out at her, wagging his whole body. He relieved himself outside while Beverly picked up the mail from the mailbox. She thumbed through the mail: bills, bills, and more bills. She hung up her jacket on one of the hooks in the garage and walked inside, with Scout close behind.

She said to Scout, "I know Laurie's going to come here with a bottle of wine so I better eat something."

She peeked into her fridge. "Pretty slim pickins, huh Scout?" she said as she rubbed behind his ears. He fell on the floor and put his paws up in the air.

"You want a belly rub, huh, boy?" She rubbed his tummy while his tail pounded on the floor.

She pulled a loaf of bread out of the freezer, grabbed two slices, and stuck them in the toaster oven. She got out the chunky peanut butter. While the bread was toasting, she went upstairs and put on her oldest pair of sweats and an old t-shirt. Scout followed her.

"No need to put anything good on if I'm going to be coloring my hair, right Scout?" He looked at her and wagged his tail. It went "thump thump". She heard the "ding" of the toaster oven just as she was putting on a pair of socks. She threw her blouse in the laundry shoot and hung up her pants. She went back downstairs and took the toast out and spread it with peanut butter. There wasn't much peanut butter left, so she scraped the bottom and sides, then gave the nearly empty plastic jar to Scout, who happily carried it over to the carpet to get better traction as he licked the inside of the jar.

She poured herself some water and sat down and opened her mail, munching her peanut- butter toast. It was a little burnt on the sides, but she barely noticed because she was so hungry. She was just finishing up her toast when the doorbell rang. Scout ran to the door barking.

"It's just Laurie, you silly dog!" she shouted as she opened the door. Scout settled down when he realized it was a friend.

Laurie had a bottle of Chardonnay in one hand and a bottle of hair coloring in the other. She held the hair-coloring box up to Beverly's head. "Yes, this will do just fine. You'll look lovely. And it's only semi-permanent, so if it really looks terrible, you can just wash it out in twelve washings."

"Right, I can do that in one night if I have to." Beverly said, laughing. "Come on in."

Beverly noticed that Laurie looked beautiful as always. She was tall, about five ten with beautiful dark brown hair in a spiky style. She looked like she was about twenty years old, even though she had a grown daughter. She was wearing jeans and a Victoria, B.C., t-shirt. She also had on a grey fleece jacket.

"When's it going to warm up around here? This is the coldest April that I can remember," Laurie said.

"Oh probably about Fourth of July, just after the Rose Festival. Probably after they take down all the rides and booths," Beverly said wistfully.

"Of course. Well, let's get to it, we have work to do," Laurie said as she came into the house, took off her shoes, and walked into the kitchen. She got out two wine glasses and the wine opener from the drawer.

Beverly said, "You know my kitchen better than I do."

"That's right." Laurie said, pouring one glass of wine and handing it to her. "This is for you. I'm not having one until after I'm done coloring your hair. I don't want to risk a hair disaster."

Beverly replied, taking a sip, "And I appreciate that. Now what do I need to do, boss?"

"Let's go to the downstairs bathroom. Don't worry, I've done this hundreds of times on myself. And believe me, it's easier doing it on somebody else for a change," she said.

"I trust you implicitly," Beverly said, emboldened by her wine.

"Now tell me about your day. I'm dying to know what happened."

"You're not going to believe it." and Beverly filled her in on finding the woman's body, how she found the bloody pipe and then it was gone, and how she searched Joe's cabinet and what she found.

"What a nutcase! And it sounds like his girlfriend, if she was his girlfriend, was just as crazy. I feel sorry for the detectives on the case. It's probably just as hard to find a killer for such a hateful person as it is for someone you wouldn't think deserved it." Laurie said. She had finished putting the gel on Beverly's hair and they went to the kitchen and sat at the table. Beverly had set the kitchen timer for thirty minutes, the duration of the coloring process.

"I'm feeling a little more awake now. I'm so glad you came over, Laurie. I've been meaning to color my hair for so long. I just haven't made an appointment," she looked at her dear friend. "And now with this whole impending divorce thing, I don't want to spend the money. I've always been afraid to color my own hair."

"I was afraid too, but once you get the right color it's a cinch. Believe me, it's not rocket science. And what I like about it is that you don't have to make an appointment and spend two hours at the hairdresser. You can just do it on your own time."

"That's a good point."

"So when is Lisa coming home?"

"Oh boy, I haven't told you the latest."

"The latest?" Laurie raised her perfectly plucked eyebrows.

"She's pregnant."

"No! Who's the father?"

"One of her scumbag professors. He's married. Surprise, surprise. And of course he won't leave his wife and family. They broke up."

Laurie's eyes opened wide.

"Oh no! I'm so sorry. Poor Lisa."

The kitchen timer went off. Laurie handed Beverly a tube of conditioner cream.

"Now take this upstairs and take a shower. Shower off all the dye—until the water runs clear. Don't shampoo. Just put on the conditioner and leave it in for at least two minutes. Then rinse that out. After your shower, we'll dry and style your beautiful hair."

While Beverly went upstairs to shower, Laurie poured herself a glass of wine and sat at the table. Beverly called to her when she was finished. "Come on upstairs!"

Beverly had taken a shower and pulled on a pair of clean jeans and a sweatshirt. She was brushing out her hair.

"I hope it doesn't look quite this dark," she said, pulling out her blow dryer."

"Oh, don't worry, hair always looks darker when it's wet."

Laurie started blowing Beverly's hair out, saying things like, "Ohhhh! This looks great!" And "Ahhhh!" She had Beverly smiling. When she finished, Beverly's hair was a lovely, light-brown color with lots of shine. Laurie had curled it under and did a little flip thing with the bangs.

Beverly gushed, "This looks so pretty. Thank you so much, I love it. Now can you come over every morning to my house and style my hair?"

"Anything for you daaahling." Laurie she said. "Now, don't wash your hair for a couple days or else you'll wash out the color too fast. You can wet your hair and style it if you want. Now let's go downstairs. I have something to tell you. I found out something about Herb," she said, a cloud passing over her face.

"I'm afraid to ask," Beverly said, walking down the stairs. They brought their wine into the living room and sat down. Beverly switched on the gas fireplace and it immediately lit up.

"Herb's girlfriend's name is Tiffany."

"I knew that. What a perfect name."

"Well, I just found out that she's pregnant." Beverly's face fell. "She's five months along."

"So really," Laurie said, "Herb's girlfriend's pregnancy can work to your advantage."

"How is that possible?" Beverly asked.

"I'm sure that she's pressuring him to get a divorce so he can marry her and give her baby a proper name."

"Oh my gosh, is this the 1950s?"

"So, if he's under time pressure, then it might be good for you to stretch it out and get everything you want."

"You think so?" Beverly said.

"Yes, I do think so. My cousin was in the same situation. Remember Mandy?" Laurie asked.

"Kind of. Didn't she get divorced about ten years ago?"

"Yep. Mandy was forty five with three kids. Her husband took up with a twenty-five- year old. The girlfriend became pregnant and wanted him to marry her right away. As a result, Mandy got a huge settlement and is sitting in the cat bird's seat."

"Yeah, but weren't Mandy's kids still at home?"

"They were, but even so, she got a big settlement on top of child support. She reminded the judge that she put him through school and was with him through the lean times. Judges *love* that. Do you have an attorney yet?"

"I got the names of two attorneys from Ruth at the senior center. Remember, I told you about Ruth? She used to be a divorce attorney."

"Is that Ruth Jamison? *The* Ruth Jamison?" Laurie asked.

"Jamison, yes—I think that's her last name."

"Oh my gosh, Beverly, she's a *legend*. She was Mandy's lawyer. She's tough as nails. She's retired?"

"Unfortunately, yes."

"Man, it's too bad you can't talk her into taking the case. How long has she been retired?"

"Not very long. Maybe six months or so, at least that's how long she's been coming to the center."

"Then maybe she still belongs to the bar association. You should ask her."

"Laurie, she's retired. She gave me two names. I'm sure they're just as good."

"Honey, nobody's as good as Ruth Jamison. You're friends, right?"

"I guess so."

"See if you can hire her. Beg her. Promise me you will."

"I'll talk with her tomorrow," Beverly said.

"Promise?"

"OK. I promise."

"I just thought of something funny."

"I can use some funny news." Beverly said.

"Herb is going to be a new father and a new grandfather, all within a few months of each other."

Chapter Nineteen

Beverly woke up to the sunshine. Even Scout seemed to know that she wanted to sleep in a little, so he didn't bug her to go out or feed him. She padded over to her chair and put on her soft lilac robe and comfy slippers. She glanced at the clock: eight thirty.

"No need to rush this morning, Scout. I don't have to get to work 'til ten. Paul's opening up."

They went downstairs, and Beverly let Scout out while she got the paper. She brought it in and sat down in her cheery, yellow kitchen. She filled up the espresso machine with water and turned it on, setting the paper on the kitchen table. "Thursday already." she said, looking down at Scout, who was sitting nicely, thinking he was going to get his kibble. "Scout, don't be such a hog. Wait until I finish my breakfast. You know I'm the top dog here, don't you?" he tilted his head in a way that made Beverly melt, but she wouldn't give in.

She pulled her cereal box out of the cabinet and poured the Raisin Bran into the bowl. Realizing that she didn't have any fruit to put in it, she started a grocery list. Bananas were at the top, and milk.

"Oh, I'm almost out of coffee beans," she said, looking into the freezer. "That would be a tragedy." She wrote down "c. beans" and peeked into the meat drawer where she kept her cheese. There was a small chunk of cheddar in there, but the cheddar was more of a green color than the usual color. She tossed it out and added it to her list.

"That's enough for now," she said, pouring the milk on her cereal.

The green light lit up on the espresso machine, so she poured some milk into the pitcher and put it under the frothing nozzle. It made satisfying hiss sounds as the milk heated up. She sat down and started eating her cereal with Scout right below her, just in case anything fell down. She remembered that a few weeks back she was eating a bagel with cream cheese and accidentally dropped it. It actually went right into Scout's mouth. He was so surprised he almost didn't know what to do. Beverly figured he was still dreaming of that moment and hoping it would repeat itself.

She knew the milk was heated up to the right temperature by the way it was hissing, so she got up and turned the nozzle off, cleaned it, and ran the espresso. She got out her port-a-cup and poured in the espresso, then grabbed the big jug of chocolate syrup from the fridge and pumped in some of the delicious chocolate. She mixed it up with a chopstick and added the steamed milk. She mixed it well and put the top on the cup. She cleaned the frothing nozzle and the area and dumped the espresso grinds into the garbage.

She sat back down and finished her cereal and read the comics. Then she fed Scout, who gobbled his kibble. Feeling refreshed, she rinsed out her bowl feeling a bit alone.

"I'm glad I have you to keep me company, Scout."

She went upstairs to get dressed and brush her teeth. When she got to the mirror she was shocked at her hair color. Overnight, she had forgotten that Laurie had colored it. She brushed it out. It seemed to be going every which way. But the color looked good. She remembered Laurie telling her not to wash it, but that she could wet and style it. She stuck her head under the sink and turned on the water. It was freezing, and she yanked her head up, bumping her head on the faucet.

"Dang it!" she said, turning the water back on to heat it up.

She waited a minute or so with cold, dripping hair until the water warmed up, and she stuck her head back under. After a couple seconds, the cold water came back in full force so she quickly wet her hair and turned off the faucet and grabbed a towel.

"Stupid plumbing!" she said.

She toweled off her hair a little and then combed it out. She selected her clothes. She wanted to cheer herself up, so she wore a bright red blouse and slimming black pants. She blew dry her hair and had to admit that she looked good, so much better than with those ugly gray roots. She applied her makeup, especially some under-eye cover. She brushed her teeth and even put on some lipstick. She was ready for the day.

The phone rang as she was doing a final brushing of her hair, and she ran over to the phone by her bed and picked it up.

"Hello?" she said.

"Hi Beverly, this is Officer Jim Swenson. I'm sorry to be bothering you at home."

She had already recognized his deep voice. Rather sexy, she thought.

"No problem. What's up? I hope not another murder?" She laughed nervously and went on, "Sorry, I didn't mean that."

"That's OK. I guess that's my business, isn't it? Anyway, I was wondering if you could help Mike and me in our investigation."

"Sure, anything."

"We were talking last night, and we thought that since you have such a good relationship with the seniors there maybe you can do a little investigating yourself—I mean, besides what you've already been doing."

Beverly sat right up, excited. "Really? Do you really think I can help besides what I've already uncovered? What do you want me to do? Do you think one of the seniors did it?"

"Well, I didn't say that. But I think that maybe someone there knew something or was somehow involved in some way with the murders. I mean, we interviewed everyone who was there at the time of the first murder, but we're thinking that maybe someone else or some other people may have some pertinent information. So, instead of us having to interview everyone at the center, we thought that you might be able to do some poking around. You know, kind of casually. I've seen you talking with the seniors, and they really like and trust you."

"What do you want me to focus on?"

"Well, since the victims both appeared to be involved in Nazi-type activities, and they seemed to be planning something at the Holocaust Museum this weekend, which just happens to be Yom HaShoah, the Day of Remembrance, we think there was probably a connection there. Maybe some of the seniors got wind of the plan, or just plain hated Joe and wanted to stop him. There may be some cover-ups going on."

"Oh, cover-ups? You think so?" she said, liking this more and more. She was feeling like Monk—the highly intelligent but obsessive-compulsive detective on TV. Maybe not, she thought smugly. The highly intelligent part fit but not the obsessive-compulsive part.

"We don't know for sure," Jim said, "But we think that it can't hurt for you to keep your eyes and ears open."

"I'd love to help." Maybe I'm more like Agatha Christie's Miss Marple, she thought. No, she's way too old. "Do you have any specifics?" she asked.

"Well, I'd like to give you a list that I put together of things to look for. I'm afraid it's probably not all inclusive. It's more like general questions that we have. Would it be possible for me to drop it by before you go to work? Or maybe we can meet for a quick cup of coffee. I called the center, and Paul said that you're planning on arriving a little late. Do you have time? I'd rather not meet at the center, as it might rouse suspicion."

"Sure, I'd be happy to meet for coffee."

They agreed to meet at a small independent coffee shop not far from the center in ten minutes.

Almost as an afterthought, Beverly went back upstairs and checked on her hair and makeup and spritzed on some perfume. She headed back downstairs and grabbed her purse and said goodbye to Scout. She got into her car and drove over to the coffee shop.

By the time she got to the shop, Jim was already there, sitting at a corner table in the front. She looked for that silver head of hair and saw him easily. He was wearing a dark-blue jacket with dark-blue pants. She also noticed that they had recently remodeled the coffee shop with new light-wooden tables and burgundy-colored, padded chairs. Since it wasn't too busy, Beverly went right to the counter and got herself a coffee and then went over to the condiment center and put lots of cream and sugar in it. She also added a sprinkle of cinnamon. She walked over to Jim and said hello.

"Hi, Beverly. Wow! You look great! Did you do something to your hair?"

"Thank you. I had it done," she said. "Now, what's my assignment, Sherlock?"

He smiled and got out his pad.

Chapter Twenty

Jim sipped his coffee and set it down.

"I've jotted down a few questions on this sheet," he said, ripping off a sheet of paper from his pad.

Beverly looked at the short list. She noted that he had very neat handwriting.

He had written: "Day of Remembrance—who knows about it? Anyone at center observing it? Does anyone know about underground Nazi fighters?"

Beverly asked, "Underground Nazi fighters?"

Jim said, "That's a reference to 'Nazi fighters.' It's the decoration given to Israelis who fought against the Nazis during World War II in the armed forces of any Allied nation or as a partisan. They were given a special Nazi fighter ribbon."

"So what's the 'underground' part?" Beverly asked.

"Well, we're not sure of its exact nature, but we think that it's a loose organization that makes its goal to make sure that the Nazis are known for what they did—the discrimination, the killings, etc. The members fight against the very active neo-Nazi movement today, but the history of Nazi fighters goes back to WWII."

"Seems like a worthwhile organization. But do you think it includes murder as a weapon against the neo-Nazis or Nazi sympathizers?" Beverly asked.

"I don't really know. Like I said, I'm just jotting things down for you to look into. I don't want to leave anything out."

"OK. Next you wrote—'See how well known it was that the keys were in the supply cabinet.' I can poke around. That should be easy enough to figure out."

"And the last thing I wrote is kind of a catch all—suspicious or changed behavior. You can look and ask around to see if anyone is behaving differently than normal. You know, like they have a secret. Or if there's anybody new at the center who's behaving strangely."

"I should be good at that, my soon to be ex-husband had been acting suspiciously for the last year or so. It was easy for me to tell, but hard for me to admit. I'll be much more objective at the center."

"I'm sorry to hear about your husband. My wife left me ten years ago. Having a spouse in law enforcement is very hard on a marriage—lots of erratic hours and worries. Now she's married to an accountant and seems very happy. But that's another subject altogether. So, do you think you might be able to poke around a little at the center and touch base with me if you find anything out?"

"Absolutely, I'd be happy to. Well, I better get over to work. Today is lunch day at the center. The lunches aren't really gourmet, but they are very popular. Maybe I'll learn something. I'll take notes but not in front of the seniors of course."

"Great. Thanks for your help."

They walked out to their cars. After they left, Laura, who was too far away to hear their conversation, made a quick phone call on her cell phone.

After a short drive, Beverly arrived at work. As she walked in, she was remembering the horrible events of the previous week. She found it amazing that at some times of the day she felt perfectly fine, in fact, she could almost forget about the murders, but then the thoughts of seeing Joe on the floor with a knife in his back came flooding back. She still couldn't believe that she actually tried to save him.

"I'm just not a very brave person, overall," she said to herself. "I don't know what came over me."

She passed Paul's office and saw that he was on the phone. She peeked in and waved hello. He gave her a big smile and pointed to his hair and gave her a thumbs up sign. She smiled, figuring that he approved of her new hair color. She continued to her office and unlocked and opened the door.

She hung up her jacket and sat down at her desk and logged on to her computer. Not much happening this morning, probably because she had taken care of most everything the previous night. There were a few things for her to do based on a couple e-mails from Paul. She smiled to herself as she thought about the way Paul worked. He thought of things quickly, and then put them in an e-mail to Beverly to take care of.

Ugh, one of the tasks today was to clean the bathrooms. Paul explained in his e-mail that with Joe gone there was nobody to take care of that. She just hoped that she wouldn't have to polish the floors. She looked down at her nice clothes and decided that she would go home for a late lunch and change into her grubby jeans. No need to ruin more of her clothes.

There was also an e-mail from Lisa. According to the e-mail she was planning on being home the next evening. Beverly remembered that she had changed the locks since Lisa was last home. She e-mailed that information back to Lisa and said that she would be sure to be home to welcome her. She sent the e-mail off and immediately got an Instant Message invitation from Lisa to have a conversation. She clicked "Yes" and saw that Lisa was already typing.

"hi mom, I figured you were online when I got your email. how r u?" she said.

"Hi Lisa. I got in late today. Laurie colored my hair. It looks much better."

"good. how r u doing with the murder and everything? r u ok?"

"I'm fine. I'm working with the police. This guy named Officer Swenson. He wants me to poke around."

"really? sounds cool. what does he want u 2 do?"

"Try to get some info from some of the seniors. Just listen, really."

"just be careful, ok mom?"

"I will. I'll see you tomorrow. About 8 or so?"

"I should be there at 8 or 8:30. sandy is going to help me pack up a few things. she said I can get the rest later."

"Maybe we can send your dad down to get the rest later on."

"good idea."

"And I don't want you lifting stuff. You need to watch your health."

"k mom, you're such a worry wart."

"I love you, honey, I'll see you tomorrow."

"bye!"

Beverly finished up the few tasks that Paul asked her to do—except cleaning the bathrooms. She decided to go into the main social room for a while. She glanced at her watch and saw they'd be serving lunch soon. Now would be a good time to start poking around. She brought out the cash box to take the money for the lunches and saw that the cash table was already set up. The volunteers were there in full force. Lunch days were busy, with the food prep and serving, and there were always a few extra volunteers on hand to help get food to the seniors who used walkers and wheelchairs. It was too hard for those people to manage the trays. Lunch officially began at eleven thirty, but the volunteers were ready for the lunch crowd by eleven fifteen, since many of the seniors got there then. Beverly set the cash box down, and Emily set up a chair behind the cash table.

Beverly remembered that Emily loved working at the cash table. She had been a cashier at various grocery stores for thirty-five years before retiring two years ago. She'd been trained on the old, non-digital cash registers that didn't calculate change. She lived in Washington State for a while at the beginning of her career, where she had to calculate and add in taxes before moving to Oregon, the land of no sales taxes. So, Emily enjoyed adding sums in her head and making change for the forty or so seniors who came to eat on lunch days. She also had a pad of paper next to her to keep track of the number of lunches she sold. At the end of the lunch shift, she carefully counted out and wrote out the amounts of cash by denomination and coin. She always cashed out to the penny, unless she had a few IOUs, which she carefully tracked. On occasion, a few of the seniors either forgot their money or needed to wait until their Social Security checks came in to pay for their lunches. That was OK with Beverly. So, once Emily was seated, she counted up the cash in the box and wrote the amount down. Beverly was then free to mingle.

A few people were already seated, not caring to buy lunches. There were several people who brought their own lunches. The lunches were usually in small coolers. Beverly found it kind of funny that several of the people had the exact same coolers. She found out later that Target had a great sale on coolers, and many of the seniors went to the store together and all bought the same style.

Beverly sat down at a table full of ladies who had their own lunches and were already eating. She saw that there was a line forming at Emily's table, but the kitchen volunteers weren't quite ready to serve yet.

"May I join you ladies?" Beverly asked.

"Of course. Come have a seat." Gladys, a friendly woman with loosely curled red hair and bright blue eyes, said, pulling out a chair next to her.

"Thanks." Beverly said, remembering that all four of them had been at the dance the night before. "Did you all enjoy the dance last night?"

Gladys said, "Oh, it was very enjoyable. I just love that band. So versatile. They really kept the crowd on their feet, didn't they, Jane?"

Jane was Gladys's best friend—a very short, plump woman with rosy cheeks and a warm smile. "If only there were more partners."

"You know," Beverly said, "it seems like nowadays everybody dances with everybody—girls with other girls, boys with boys. I was so shocked when I chaperoned at one of my daughter's high school dances. It seemed like they were just dancing all in big groups."

Jane tittered, "But I bet it would be hard to do the tango in a group."

The ladies chuckled.

"I saw that even Paul was out there cutting the rug," Beverly said.

Gladys said, "I danced a waltz with him. He's so smooth. Especially for such a young man. Seems like a lot of the young men today only know how to dance that hip hop."

Jane said, "I wish my granddaughter didn't live in Chicago. I'd introduce her to Paul in a heartbeat. He needs a nice girl. He doesn't have a girlfriend, does he, Beverly?"

Beverly replied, slightly disconcerted, "Uh—I don't think so. I kind of see him as a confirmed bachelor. You know, some men are, like Nathan Small. He was here last night, wasn't he?"

Gladys responded, "Oh, he's a marvelous dancer. And a good-looking man, if I do say so myself. But he's not a confirmed bachelor. He's a widower."

"Oh, I didn't know that. He hasn't been coming to the center for very long, has he? I don't remember seeing him until probably three months ago."

Gladys said, "You're right. I think he's been coming here for two months if that. He just moved to the neighborhood. He used to live a bit farther, but he bought a small house nearby. I'm surprised he hasn't been snatched up."

"Me too, he's a dreamboat" Betsy, sitting to Gladys' right, added.

"Does he ever come to the lunches? I think I've seen him, but I'm not sure," Beverly asked.

Betsy answered, "I've seen him at a few of the lunches I think, but I'm not positive about that. Do you remember Jane?"

Jane said, "Let me think." She paused. "I do believe he's been to a few, but he definitely is not a regular. Oh look." She tried to indicate the doorway without pointing. "Speak of the devil. Looks like he's coming for lunch today."

"I'll have to introduce myself. I haven't had the pleasure of speaking with him yet," Beverly said, looking at Nathan.

He was dressed in a perfectly pressed pair of khaki pants and a short-sleeved polo shirt. He looked like he had just come from the golf course. She assumed that he had taken off his jacket and hung it up on the coat rack outside the door to the central room. She continued chatting with the ladies at the table as he walked in, paid his money, and got himself some lunch.

It was funny for Beverly to watch many of the ladies who were already seated primping, looking toward Nathan, and waving him over. He sat at the closest table to the front, not wanting to choose. He sat next to a man who had already finished his coffee, and Beverly came up and sat at the table. After saying hello to the regulars, she introduced herself to Nathan.

"Hello, my name is Beverly Clavel. I'm the assistant to the director here at the center," she held out her hand.

"My name is Nathan Small," he said, politely standing and taking her hand. "I just started coming here a few months ago. It's a very nice center."

"Thank you. Nathan. Are you new in the area?"

"Yes and no; I've lived in Portland for many years, but I recently moved nearby to be closer to my daughter and grandkids," he said.

"Do you live with your daughter?" she asked.

"Oh no," he said with a laugh. "That would be a little too close. But I took a small house about two blocks from her."

"I'll bet she loves having you close by," she said.

"I think so. I try to help out. She just got divorced, you see, and my grandchildren are school aged," he said. "So I try to help out where I can."

"That's great. I mean, not that she just got divorced, but it's great that you are helping out," she stammered, and changed the subject quickly, "I saw that you were at the dance last night. Did you enjoy it?" she asked.

"Yes. The band was very good. I especially like to waltz, and they played a wonderful 'Blue Danube.'"

"Well I'll be sure to tell the band. They seem to get a kick out of playing here."

"I guess there isn't too much call for the type of music that I like these days."

"You'd be surprised. Rosie and the Boys are quite popular and busy around town." She said. "And they are really great to work with. Nathan, are you retired?"

"I guess you could say I'm semi-retired. I don't think I could ever be truly retired. I consult every now and then." He said.

"Oh really? My daughter has expressed an interest in being a consultant, but I think she needs to become an expert in some field before she can do that."

"Well, I wouldn't call myself an expert, but I have a lot of real-estate development experience, so that's what I work on."

"Oh, that must be interesting. Do you work with the developers or the investors or what?" she asked, trying to keep him talking.

"Mainly the developers; you'd be amazed at the complexity of some of the deals."

"It sounds very interesting. Well, it certainly was nice meeting you Nathan. I hope to see you often. I better get back to work now," she said goodbye to the rest of the people at the table, who were engrossed in their own conversations.

"It was my pleasure," he said, standing when she stood up.

Beverly made her way back through the crowd, saying hello, asking how the food was, making sure the non-ambulatory folks had enough to drink. Then, she went down the hall and to her office. She was shocked to see a big sheet of paper taped to her computer that said, "WATCH YOUR BACK" in big, bold, red letters.

Chapter Twenty One

Beverly gasped when she saw the "WATCH YOUR BACK" sign on her computer. She thought about the knife in Joe's back and immediately dug through her purse, found the card she was looking for, picked up the phone, and called Officer Swenson. She felt like she needed to put his phone number on speed dial, seeing how much she'd been talking with him lately.

"Officer Swenson," he answered.

"Officer, this is Beverly Clavel. I—I just got back to my office and there was a sign that said 'watch your back' taped to my computer. It was written in big red letters. It looks like somebody used fat markers. I'm really scared."

"I'll be right over. Don't touch anything."

"But I touched the phone" she said.

"That's OK, just get out of your office. Go to the central room there. I'll be at the front door in ten minutes."

"Alright. I'll be waiting for you. Should I lock my door?"

"No, just go somewhere where there are lots of people around. I'm on my way," he hung up the phone.

She went over to the main room and tried hard to act naturally and to socialize with the guests as if nothing had happened. It was hard. Many of the seniors had finished their lunches and were lingering over coffee. There were a few ad hoc card games going on and there were a few people working on a jigsaw puzzle at the back of the room. Beverly looked over to the jigsaw puzzle. She always had one set up at the back table. Many people liked to do jigsaw puzzles once in a while but not all the time, so it was fun for them to just go to the back table and work on the puzzle for fifteen minutes or so then go back to their other business.

Beverly went over to the jigsaw puzzle and tried to relax. She put together a few pieces. It was a new puzzle of an American eagle with a flag in the background. It was 3-D and kind of tricky. Unfortunately for Beverly, all of the side pieces were already assembled, so only the more difficult inside pieces remained. Her hands were shaking a little so she tried to take deep breaths.

Emily, the cash table volunteer came over.

"We sold fifty-three lunches today!" she exclaimed.

"Did we have enough food?" Beverly asked.

"We did. The volunteers bought extra. They figured that because of all of the excitement this week there'd be lots of people in today."

"I think I can go for a little less excitement, thank you very much!" Beverly said, trying to find the white pieces of the jigsaw puzzle that would make up the eagle's head. Emily found one for her and she put them with the other white pieces, and then tried to make sense of them, but couldn't figure out how they fit together.

"Did everything cash out correctly?"

"To the penny. I took the cash box over to Paul in his office. Oh, and you need to order some paper towels for the kitchen. Madge told me she checked in the supply cabinet and there was only half a box left."

"Good. Thanks. I'm sure Paul will want me to make the deposit later today," she said and then saw Jim standing by the front door. "Oh and by the way Emily, I know that you and the other volunteers know where the supply cabinet is, but do others know about it also?"

"Everybody knows where the supplies are. Seniors are forever getting one thing or another. Mostly toilet paper and such. You know, Joe wasn't the greatest at keeping the ladies room supplied. Oh look over there," she said pointing to Jim, "There's that handsome police officer! If only I were twenty years younger—or maybe if he were twenty years older," she said dreamily.

Beverly said, "Hey, nothing wrong with having a younger man. We women outlive men anyway. I need to go talk with him," she said, waving to him, "and I'll make a note to myself to order some more paper towels. I'll talk with you later, Emily. Thanks again for your help," she said.

Emily said, "You should ask him out, Beverly. Don't wait for him to ask."

"Bye, Emily," she said, feeling her face heat up, and walked over to meet Jim.

"Hi, Beverly, how 'bout we take a look at that sign," he said.

"It certainly took me by surprise," she said, leading him to her office. He was carrying a large ziplock bag. When they got to the office, he looked at the note silently. He took out a pair of gloves and put them on. He carefully pulled the note off of the computer, making sure he didn't rip the tape. He put the note into the bag.

"Do you think the CSI team needs to dust for fingerprints?" she said, trying to hide the anxiety in her voice.

He tried to hide his smile. "I really don't think it will do much good. If there are any fingerprints, they'll be on the tape or the note."

"Oh yes, of course. You're right. Let me get you a chair so you can sit down." There were a couple plastic chairs in the hallway so she pulled one in. It barely fit in her small office. He sat down on the one small chair in front of Beverly's desk. He put the ziplock bag on the floor and looked around her office.

"Is that your daughter?" he said, pointing to a large picture on the wall.

"Yes. That was her high school graduation picture. She's in college now, or I guess I should say she was in college."

"She's a lovely girl. I can definitely see the resemblance. Did she graduate from college recently?"

"No, she's in her second year. But she just decided to take some time off, so she's coming home this weekend. It will be strange having her home."

"I imagine so. I've lived alone for so long that it would be a hard adjustment if someone were living with me I think. I don't have kids, but I have a nephew who's taking a year off from college. I sure hope he does go back next year as planned. Sometimes they lose focus, you know."

"That's very true. But I think you're changing the subject. Who do you think left this note?"

"That's a good question, Beverly. I have a few theories, but none of them are very definite. Maybe somebody saw us at the coffee shop together, or maybe somebody didn't want you helping the victim in the first place. There's even a possibility that someone may be targeting the center employees."

Beverly gasped, "You think so? But it's just me and Paul left. Do you really think that's possible?"

"You know, in my business anything's possible. But I don't think that's very likely. I can't imagine a scenario where somebody was so disgruntled with the senior center that they'd want to take all of its employees out. Unless you know something that I don't."

Beverly pondered for a moment. "The only thing I can think of is something that happened three, maybe, four months ago."

"Really?" he said, taking out his pad of paper and pen.

"Yes. There was an incident where the son of one of our seniors had gotten into a big fight with his mother, I believe it had to do with money, and he started scaring and kind of stalking her."

He started writing. "Who was it?"

"Her name is Kat Orton. I think her full name is Katherine Orton, but everybody calls her Kat."

"Does she still attend functions here?"

"Yes, she does. She's always been very active, and I'm glad that she feels comfortable being here again. Anyway, about three months ago her son started coming here every time she was here. He would sneak in and sit at the back of the room where she was and just stare at her. She saw him immediately but didn't usually say anything for a while. You see, we can't really turn people away here. So even though technically he wasn't a senior, we couldn't kick him out. But then others started to notice and provided her protection. You know, like surrounding her and blocking him off. Finally, she came to me and told me of the situation. I talked with Paul about it, and he said that it was perfectly acceptable to kick him out."

"Did you talk with the son then?"

"Yes, I told him that he had to leave, that he was being disruptive to the seniors and especially to Mrs. Orton. Well, he left, but just for that day. He was back the very next day. I didn't know what to do, so I talked with Paul again. Well, Paul is not too big on conflict, but he knew he had to do something. So he talked with Orton and threatened to get a police order against him if he showed up again."

"Did that do the trick?"

"We thought so. He didn't come back for about a week or so. But then he was back. Some of the seniors had told me that Mrs. Orton had changed her will and left him nothing. She kind of disowned him. I'm not sure if that's true. Anyway, he was gone and we were happy, and then all of the sudden he showed up again."

"Oh, boy," he commiserated.

"By then, Joe Boulden had gotten wind of the situation. Even though Joe was kind of a jerk, he didn't like the fact that the guy was harassing his own mother. He started noticing when he would come in to stare at poor Kat. So one day, Joe went up to him and grabbed the back of his shirt—and Kat's son was a pretty big guy. Well, Joe basically dragged the guy out the door. I wasn't there and neither was Paul, but several seniors were coming in to the center at the time. There was a lot of swearing going on, and Joe basically told the guy to leave his mother alone and to f-off, if you know what I mean. I heard that Joe punched him in the face, and he was bleeding but he left and never came back."

"And Kat Orton. Does she still come here, even after the incidents?"

"Yes, she does. In fact she's here today if you want to talk with her."

"Yes, I believe I would."

"Oh, I just thought of something. The woman I met with on the day of the murder, the woman who was selling the copy machine, her name is Terri Orton. I wonder if they're related."

Chapter Twenty Two

Jim and Beverly continued to talk in Beverly's tiny office.

Jim said, "There could possibly be a connection between the copy-machine salesperson and the son who was bothering his mother. That's true. Orton isn't a very common name."

Beverly replied, "And it always comes down to money, right? Seems like whenever I watch a detective show, money is *always* involved when there's a murder. But I guess passion is a close second, and hate is a pretty big passion."

"Money is usually a big motivator in murder cases," Jim agreed, "But not always."

Beverly said, "And if Kat was changing her will and disowning her son, maybe Terri was his son's wife. And then I'm sure that Terri would have suffered by not having the money too."

Jim countered, his pen paused, "But do you know for sure that Terri was Kat's daughter-in-law?"

She waited a moment. "No, I guess not. I'm speculating." She paused. "But that's what detectives do, don't they? They speculate."

"That's true, they do speculate. And Mike and I will definitely follow up with Kat Orton and Terri Orton to see what they have to say. And I'll find out more about who Kat's son is and question him. Do you have any idea how much money might have been in her will?"

"All I know is that Kat is always elegantly dressed and wears jewelry, even to the most casual events at the center. And her hair and nails are always done. And you know that doesn't come cheap."

"I suppose not," he said.

Jim's phone rang.

"Excuse me," he said to Beverly, and then said "Swenson here," into the phone.

Beverly listened in, but the one-sided conversation meant little to her. Jim talked for a few minutes and hung up.

"That was Mike. He just got the report from the coroner regarding the woman's murder. She was shot twice in the back of the head and appeared to be dragged. Mike figures the murderer dragged her to a less populated part of the parking lot, just like we thought."

"Oh, man. I forgot about her. Why would Kat's son kill that girl too? I have to think there's a connection between Joe and the girl. I guess my theories aren't holding much water, are they?"

"I honestly can't say. We always have to keep our minds open. I guess we just have to do some more digging. Did you find anything out from the list of questions I gave you?"

"Well, I was just starting to poke around with the seniors a bit before I went back to my office. There's one fellow named Nathan Small who started coming here a few months back. I just wanted to see what his background was. I know it probably doesn't make a difference, but I had heard that another senior had served on a committee with him at the local synagogue, so I thought there might be a 'Nazi fighter' connection. But I didn't come up with much. He's a semi-retired real-estate developer. He still does some consulting. He recently moved to be closer to his daughter and grandkids. Now he lives pretty close to the center, so he's able to come more often."

"Hmmm," Jim said, writing down a few notes.

"Wait a minute. Paul's partner, Wes, is a real-estate developer Maybe he knows Nathan Small."

"We have talked with Wes. It seems a bit far-fetched that there's a connection there, but I'll make a note of it."

"So what do you want me to do, Kojak? Oh, I guess I can't call you Kojak since you have too much hair." she said.

"You can call me Jim. That would probably be best," he smiled.

He had one of those smiles that lit up his whole face in an infectious kind of way. Beverly grinned back and hoped her cheeks weren't flushed as she tried to stop staring at his eyes and listen to what he was saying.

"Now tell me, since you've been threatened, you need to consider your own safety. Do you have a security system at home?"

"Well, yes and no. I have a security system installed, but when my husband left, I stopped paying for surveillance. I'm trying to save money. So it's not really hooked up to any service anymore."

"Oh."

"But I do have a dog, a black lab/shepherd mix, and he's very protective. He barks at everyone. I feel very safe with him."

"That's good. I think dogs are often more intimidating to criminals than security systems."

"I agree. I adopted him two months ago, and he's been a great dog."

"You said that your daughter will be coming home from college soon. Is there anyone else in the house now?"

"No, just me and Scout—Scout's the dog."

"You need to be especially vigilant at home. Lock your windows and doors. And here at the center make sure you are never the only one in here. If you have to lock up at night make sure Paul or a volunteer is with you. Be careful in the parking lot too. You might want to start parking up front near the door. And feel free to call me anytime, day or night," he pulled out one of his cards and wrote a phone number on the back. "Here's my cell phone number. I have it on all of the time. If you feel the least bit threatened, call me. You might want to put the number on speed dial, just in case."

"OK, and one other thing, Jim."

"Yes, what is it?"

"I checked with one of my volunteers and she said that everybody knew about the supply cabinet—not just the volunteers but most of the seniors as well. I guess Joe was forever forgetting to fill up the toilet paper supply in the ladies room. Oh, that reminds me. I have bathroom duty today, so I get to clean the bathrooms. I need to go home and change."

"Bathroom duty? Is that what the assistant to the director does?"

"Not normally, but with Joe gone somebody has to do it. And Paul isn't going to don the rubber gloves and clean toilets here while wearing one of his beautiful silk shirts, that's for sure."

"You know, I can't really see Paul doing that either. Just be careful and call me if you need me," Jim said, and walked out of Beverly's office while she watched his back. She was thinking that she liked the way his pants fit him. And she could see his broad shoulders through his shirt.

After he left, she did program his cell phone number on her speed dial. He was number three, behind Lisa and her own voice-mail number. Feeling pathetic that she only had three speed-dial numbers programmed, Beverly went back to the main room to chat with a few of the seniors to see how things were going.

After checking in with a few people, she walked back to Paul's office and said, "I'm going to head home for a late lunch and I'll change into jeans so I can clean the bathrooms."

"I appreciate you doing that. It will probably be at least a few weeks before I get authorization to hire a new custodian. There's always so much red tape. Anyway, I'm here all day, so no problem you going to lunch. We should probably check with each other whenever we plan to head out of the building just so one of us is here all the time," Paul added.

"I agree. One of us needs to always be available," Beverly said, and then remembered the early morning opening up duties. "Maybe we can split up the early morning duty."

Paul said, "Sounds good. We can talk about it early next week. Have a good lunch."

Beverly waved and headed back to her office to grab her purse and jacket. She knew that Paul wouldn't want the early-morning duty because he was generally not a morning person.

She drove home and pulled into the driveway. She could hear happy cries from Scout. She got out of the car and opened the side door between the garage and the house. Scout came bounding out, butt wiggling a mile a minute.

"Go on out, Scout," she said, setting her purse on the floor in the kitchen. She walked out to the mailbox. Nothing but ads.

At least there aren't any bills today, she thought, walking back to the house. Scout came in after, her and she closed the garage door and went inside.

She saw that she had a voice mail because her phone was flashing. "I'll get it in a minute, Scout, won't I boy?" she said, petting his head. He sat and his tail thumped happily on the floor. She went upstairs and changed into jeans and a sweatshirt. She knew that while it was a little bit sunny outside, it was still cold. But then she thought again and realized that cleaning toilets and long sleeves didn't go together, so she put on an old t-shirt. She caught her reflection in the mirror and almost gasped at the change in her hair color. It was always so shocking at first.

"But it looks good, doesn't it boy?" she said to Scout. He appeared to shake his head "yes."

She went back downstairs and got herself a scoop of peanut butter and some yogurt for lunch. She sat down and finished the paper. When she was done, she listened to her voice mail. It was Herb.

"I don't know why you don't want to participate in mediation. What's wrong with you? If we have to both get lawyers and drag this out, we'll just spend more and more money. Be reasonable, Beverly. Call me."

Since she was now armed with insider information—the fact that Herb's girlfriend was five months pregnant—she knew that Herb was very motivated to settle and that now she had a better chance of a good settlement. And she also knew that Herb had an attorney already who was watching out for his interests. *Maybe I should go to Ruth Jamison to see if she'll make an exception to her retirement and take me on as a client* she thought, picking up her phone book and looking up Ruth's number.

Fortunately, Ruth was home. Beverly pled her case, and Ruth said, "I'm really not taking any cases. In fact, my bar membership is considered inactive, so I couldn't really practice law even if I wanted to. But I would be happy to consult with you on this. And I'm telling you, I've personally trained the woman, Lynn Baker, whose name I gave you earlier. She'll do a good job for you," Ruth said.

"OK, I guess that will have to do. And I just found out from my friend that Herb's girlfriend is pregnant."

"That's good news, at least from a certain standpoint. He'll probably be under time pressure. That can really work to your advantage, Beverly."

"That's what I was thinking or at least hoping. Anyhow, I'll call Lynn right now."

"Just tell her I sent you and that I want to be involved with the case," Ruth added.

"OK. I'll call her right away. And thanks again, Ruth," she hung up and called Lynn.

The attorney was with a client at the time, but the administrative assistant took Beverly's name and number and said, "Well, if Ruth referred you, I'm sure she'll get back to you just as soon as she's free."

Beverly thanked her and hung up. "I better get back to work, Scout. I've got toilets to clean."

Chapter Twenty Three

Beverly decided there was no point in putting off the inevitable. It was time to tackle the restrooms. Thinking the men's room was probably messier, she began there, wanting to get it over with first. She took the cleaning supplies into the restroom and set up shop, hoping that nobody would come in while she was cleaning. There were three urinals and two stalls in the bathroom.

I've never cleaned a urinal before, she thought. *But I guess it's important to learn new skills. Come to think of it, I've never actually flushed a urinal either.* She flushed the urinals, and then squirted the toilet bowl cleaner on them. She flushed the two toilets then and squirted the toilet bowl cleaner around the bowl. She figured she better move fast on one toilet so as to have one that was usable quickly. She scrubbed it hard and left the chemical in there to soak. She got the mop and mopped up the floor in the stall and made a mental note to herself to get some more toilet paper.

She moved back to the urinals when a man entered the room. It was Paul. He didn't notice her as he unzipped his fly. In his haste to get to the urinal, he bumped right into her.

"What the heck. I'm sorry." he said. "Beverly, it's you!"

Beverly turned and hurried out the door. Paul—red faced—came out of the restroom soon thereafter and barged past Beverly, trying to pretend nothing had happened.

After that flustering encounter, Beverly propped the door of the restroom open and cleaned everything up in double time. She had a new appreciation for custodians, realizing for herself what hard work it was. She used the toilet-bowl brush to brush out the urinals and flushed them a few times. She cleaned the other toilet. She cleaned out the three sinks and checked to see that there was soap in the dispensers. She cleaned the mirror next and then started to mop rest of the floor when Rod, the former bankruptcy attorney, walked in.

"Oh, you're in here Beverly!"

"Yes, I'm sorry. I just need to mop the floor and I'm done. But I'm happy to step out."

"I'd appreciate that if you don't mind. My prostate just isn't like it used to be."

"Of course, I'll get out of your way," she said and stepped out with the caddy of cleaning equipment and moved it over to the ladies room. She was thinking that the men's room was really very clean even before she deep cleaned it, and then she remembered that it probably wasn't used all that much since there were fewer men than women at the center.

She went back to the men's room just as Rod was walking out.

"Thanks Beverly," he said.

"No problem. There's nobody else in there, is there?"

"Nope, the coast is clear."

She went back in and quickly finished mopping the floor. It was hard because the mop was really heavy. She then went back to the women's room. There were four stalls in there and she noticed that one of the toilets seemed to be running constantly. It was the furthest stall from the door so she went over there and jiggled the handle. She waited a bit, but it still didn't seem to be filling up and stopping. So she lifted the back tank lid and set it on the seat. There was something in the tank that was blocking the mechanism that wouldn't allow the flap to close and let the water fill up and stop. She saw it was the missing metal bar that she had found under the classroom table—the one with the blood on it. She stifled an exclamation and hurried out to her office to get her phone.

She dialed speed dial number three. Officer Jim Swenson answered right away.

"You're not going to believe this!" Beverly exclaimed, and then explained what she found in the toilet tank.

"Mike and I will be right over," he said and hung up.

When Jim and Mike showed up in Beverly's office, she said, "I'll show you where I saw the pipe or whatever it was."

"Hope it hasn't disappeared this time," Mike said, trying to stifle a laugh.

"Very funny," Beverly said and glared at him.

The two cops followed her to the restroom, and Mike had the decency to look a little sheepish.

When they got to the ladies room, Beverly put on her rubber gloves and lifted the toilet tank cover off and pointed inside.

"There it is. I think it's the same metal bar that I saw the other day under the classroom table."

They both looked in.

Jim said, "I better call the CSI team to see what they want me to do with it. I doubt there is much evidence left on the bar itself after being in the water, but they may want to dust for prints on the tank."

"Well, I have good news," Beverly said. "I was wearing rubber gloves when I lifted up the cover the first time, so my prints shouldn't be all over the place for a change."

"At least we have that going for us" Jim replied. He left the restroom to make his phone call. Meanwhile, two women stepped into the ladies room and were startled when they saw big, burly Mike Petrovsky inside. They took their leave.

One of them said, "I'll come back later."

Jim completed his phone call and returned to talk to Beverly.

"They want to send out one of their techs to pick up the evidence and dust for prints. But she can't get here for an hour," he said.

Beverly said, "I'm glad that they're sending a woman to work in the ladies room because then we don't have to close it up. I'll just shut the stall door and put an Out of Order sign on it."

Jim said, "Do you have a few minutes to talk?"

"Sure," Beverly said. "Are you kidding? That means I get to postpone bathroom duty for a little while longer. We can go into one of the classrooms. Let me just write the Out of Order sign and get some tape. Then I'll get my keys. You wait here." She went to her office for the supplies and keys and came back to the restroom. When she got back, there were three women flirting outrageously with the police officers. *Word had gotten around*, she said to herself with a sigh.

She went to the back stall and taped up the sign, and then she realized that she would have to lock the stall from the inside and then crawl under the stall to get out.

Not a chance of that happening, she thought to herself. Instead of locking the door the proper way, she just taped it shut. She figured with the Out of Order sign, nobody would try to push it open, and it would hold for an hour or so until the technician showed up.

"OK ladies, you can use the restroom now. Thank you so much for being patient."

"No problem," said Gladys, who'd been the worst flirting offender. "It was our pleasure," she said, winking at Jim. Jim looked sufficiently embarrassed as Jim and Beverly walked over to the classroom.

Gladys said to her friend, "Ah, if I was only twenty years younger."

Her friend tartly replied, "More like thirty."

After they shut the door, Mike said, "Those women sure are bold, aren't they?"

Jim said, "You're lucky to have anybody flirting with you with that mug."

"Boys, boys! Let's play nicely, now. What do you need to ask me?" Beverly said.

Jim regained his composure.

"The last time I spoke with you, you had received the threatening note. I imagine that you haven't had too much of an opportunity to visit with any of the seniors since then, so I want to know a bit more now about the restroom."

"Yes, that was a surprise, wasn't it?" she said.

"So nobody complained about the constant running of that back toilet?" Mike asked.

"No, surprisingly nobody did. And I saw the pipe under the table Tuesday. So that toilet may have been running for a couple days. I know I didn't notice it."

Mike said, "It's possible that the pipe was in a spot where it wasn't interfering with the plumbing, and then somebody used the toilet, flushed it, and then the pipe moved and impeded the flap."

"That's quite possible." Beverly said. "Toilets are funny. I have this mystery toilet in my upstairs bathroom. I call it the ghost toilet because all of the sudden for no real reason it will start to run, run, run. I've had it fixed half a dozen times. But I guess this is different."

Mike looked at her, a little bit baffled, "Uh, yeah, I think this is different."

Jim said, "Anyway, I'd like to put together a timetable for this week's events, and we can fill in everything we can. Let's work on it now while we wait for the CSI technician."

"OK." Beverly said. "I'll be the scribe, and that way you can write notes in your beloved notebook there. I'll write on the whiteboard."

She chose a few different colored markers and erased the board. She wrote Tuesday, Wednesday, and Thursday and drew parallel vertical lines between each entry.

Under Tuesday, she wrote in big red letters: Joe killed. Seniors find body. BC pulls out knife (she shivered as she wrote this), turns him over and tries to revive him.

Jim said, "OK, let's brainstorm and write down everything we know about what happened that day. First of all, Joe had to unlock the doors, open up, turn on lights, etc."

Beverly wrote that down.

She said, "Paul was in the office early, but then he left for an appointment. He stopped by my office just before the meeting and gave me a spreadsheet—you know, things to look for in a new copy machine."

Beverly wrote, "Paul in early, left for meeting."

"Let's try to put some times in here, at least for Tuesday," Jim said.

Beverly said, "I know I got in right at eight thirty. I had to pick up something for my mother's birthday at the grocery store. I got her a card and a plant and left it in my car."

She wrote down, "BC arrives 8:30."

"And I got a call from the copy machine salesperson at eight forty five or so, just after I got in. She was in the parking lot ready for our appointment. She was a little early, as I recall. Her name is Terri Orton."

She wrote down, "TO arrives 8:50. TO meets BC 8:55."

"I know we went to the classroom, then I left and got us coffee, probably about nine o'clock. That's when I heard the screaming."

She wrote down, "9:00 BC hears screaming."

"I ran over to where the commotion was, and that's when I saw Joe, face down with a knife in his back. I checked for a pulse and felt a slight one."

She wrote, "9:00 BC finds Joe, tries to revive, 911 called."

Jim said, "Let's back up and figure out Joe's schedule for the morning. When did he get in?"

"Well, normally he got in at six thirty, and then he opened the front door at about seven. He usually started a coffee pot too. Not for the seniors necessarily, but more so he could have his coffee in the morning."

She wrote down, "JB arrives 6:30, does morning tasks. 7:00 opens front door."

"And when do the seniors start arriving in the morning?" Mike asked, looking back at his notes.

"They usually start coming in at seven. We have many early risers, and they like to come in to get their coffee with and be with their friends."

She wrote, "Srs arrive 7:00."

Beverly said, "And we're not sure what time Paul arrived. I know he's not much of an early bird, but I did see him shortly before my meeting with Terri. Oh, wait a minute. Each day, he sends me a few e-mails letting me know what I need to do. I think he thinks of things free association, and then he'll send them to me piecemeal, just to make sure they get done. I could check my e-mail records."

Jim said, "Does Paul only have a computer here? Or can he log on from home or anywhere else?"

"He has a laptop, and he takes it everywhere. He's one of those people who likes to type notes on his computer. You know, he's still in his twenties. My daughter does the same thing. She takes her laptop to all of her classes and takes notes on it. I don't think she bought any spiral notebooks during her whole college career." Beverly said.

Mike said, "So he could have sent you e-mail from anywhere really, even the local coffee shop?"

"Yes, you're right. So I guess it wouldn't do any good to check my e-mail records."

"It couldn't hurt. And I'll check to see what time he said he was here that morning."

Beverly wrote, "PG in time?"

"Mike, you have a list of the seniors who were here that morning, right? Why don't you name them off?" Jim said.

He did, and Beverly jotted the names down.

"But really," she said, "this might not be a complete list because people are free to come and go as they please at the center. There may have been a few people that came in for coffee and left before all of this happened."

"True," Jim said, "but at least this is a start."

"After the EMTs got there, everything happened so fast—you guys came and then the CSI team." Beverly said.

Jim said, "Yes, you don't have to write all that down. Just write the approximate time—probably 9:10—EMTs, Law enforcement arrive, etc. We can check that out with our records and the EMT records."

She wrote, "9:10."

She said, "I also remember that I asked the seniors who had arrived after nine a.m. to leave, so we could question everyone who'd been there. I guess anybody could have slipped out then."

"That's true," Mike said. "Now when did Paul come back in?"

"I think it was about ten fifteen."

She wrote that down and asked, "Do either of you have that in your notes?"

"Yes," Mike said, "That matches with my notes. Now where was Terri Orton during this time?"

"She was meeting with me in the classroom, and then I went to get coffee. I think she came out when I didn't come back for a bit to check on me. She probably couldn't hear the scream. But I do remember after the EMTs came and took over, I saw her. She was part of the crowd that was watching. She was questioned and then left shortly thereafter."

"So he must have been stabbed sometime between seven and nine a.m.."

She wrote that down.

"Unless in the unlikely event that somebody was in waiting for him, or somehow followed him in at six thirty. But it couldn't have been before seven, before he opened the doors." Jim said. "Unless he opened up the front doors early that morning or somebody broke in. There's no way for us to know unless some of the seniors said they got in before seven. And anybody could really slip in unnoticed and slip out unnoticed at that time. I think we have the pertinent information for Tuesday. Let's move on to Wednesday." Jim added.

Beverly poised her marker over Tuesday when her cell phone rang.

"Excuse me," she said.

"Hello?" she said. "Oh hi, Mom. I'm in the middle of an important meeting right now, can I call you back?"

Vivian said, "Oh honey, I just wanted to ask you if you really liked Stan, you know, from our lunch on Tuesday."

She said quietly, "Mom, he was fine, but a little old for me." She saw Mike raising his eyebrows at Jim.

Vivian said, "Well, I wanted to check with you. Because if you really liked him, I wouldn't even consider this. Well, we really hit it off, and, well, he asked me out to dinner at the club tomorrow night. I said yes, but I wanted to check with you to make sure it's OK. Because, you know, I can cancel."

"Mom, that's fine with me. I really have to go." She closed the phone, red faced.

"How old do you have to be when your mother stops trying to run your life?" she asked.

Jim and Mike chuckled.

Mike said, "It'll never happen. My mother keeps trying to get me to take a less dangerous job. She's been saying that to me for ten years. Now let's move on to Wednesday. Why don't you outline what happened first thing in the morning."

Beverly went back to the whiteboard. "So Wednesday was a very eventful day also. I found the pipe with the blood on it in the classroom, under the table. Normally, I wouldn't open up those classrooms, but there was a bigger than normal crowd of people there, wanting to know the scoop about the murder. So I got in at seven and opened up the front doors immediately. I think I started pulling out chairs from the classrooms at about seven thirty, when I was told we needed some."

She wrote down. "7:00 BC arrives, 7:30 BC finds pipe.

"And then you got here in about ten minutes, and we went back to the room and the pipe was gone," She said as she wrote "7:40 Pipe gone."

"Have you heard anything about that from the CSI team?"

"Not yet, because that's the day that we found the other victim's body, and they have been busy with two cases at once," Mike said.

"Yes, what time did that murder occur again?" Beverly said, green marker poised.

Mike shuffled through his notes. "Looks like we were called at three thirty. You pretty much figured her to be the friend of Joe right away, didn't you?"

"Yes, when I saw her hair."

Beverly wrote down "3:30" and said, "What was Bethany's last name?"

"Jones, Bethany Jones."

She wrote, "BJ found dead at grocery store lot."

Then she said, "Here at the center we were getting ready for the dance."

She wrote, "5:30-8:30 p.m. Dance at Sr Center."

"And I found the bomb making instructions in Joe's work area," she said, and wrote that down.

Mike added, "And we found the e-tickets for her and Joe to Washington, D.C., for this weekend in her purse. Don't forget that."

"Oh right." She wrote that down. "Did I miss anything else for Wednesday?"

"If we think of anything, we can go back. Let's move to today," Jim said. "What happened this morning?"

"I arrived here late, about ten o'clock. Paul agreed to open up early. Jim, you and I discussed gathering information over coffee."

She wrote down their arrival times.

"Then, I talked with some of the seniors, poked around a bit, and I went back to my office and found the 'Watch your Back' sign. Jim came over and took the sign. Then, I took a late lunch to go home to change. When I got back to the center, I started cleaning and then found the pipe in that toilet tank. Let me put some times on that."

She wrote, "7:00 PG arrives, opens up; 9:00 JS and BC meet at coffee shop; 10:00 BC arrives at Center; 11:00 BC finds threatening note; 11:15 JS collects note; 2:30 BC finds pipe in toilet tank. "There we are, up to date," she said. "Did I miss anything?"

Jim said, "Not that I can think of. I've been copying down the entries in my notebook. Why don't you go ahead and erase it now, just to be on the safe side."

Jim's phone rang. After talking for a moment and hanging up he said, "The technician is here. I told her to meet us out front."

They met her and took her back to the ladies room. Beverly noticed her nametag said "Jane Kendall." She was a smallish woman, about five feet, two inches and maybe a hundred and twenty pounds. She had light brown hair with blue eyes.

She went to work, and Jim and Mike said they would like to look around a bit and then head back to the police station, while Beverly stayed with the CSI technician and shooed away many ladies who she figured probably didn't really have to use the bathroom but wanted to see what was going on.

While she worked, Beverly asked Jane , "Do you think there's anything left on the pipe after it was in the water?"

She replied, "You never know. Obviously, I would have preferred this to be dry," she said, as she lifted out the pipe from the tank and into a special plastic box. She pulled off her gloves and put on a dry pair. She set aside the box and put the tank lid back on and started dusting for fingerprints on the top of the tank, which had remained dry. Beverly watched.

"I would think that your work is very interesting. Do you like it?" she asked.

"Yes, I do very much. I'm very detail oriented, and I like to think of myself as a mystery solver," Jane said.

"Did it take much training?" Beverly asked.

"Well, I have a college degree, and then I went to the police academy. I decided quickly that I wasn't cut out to be a cop, so I specialized in this work," Jane replied.

"Seems fascinating," Beverly said.

"Well, like any other job, it has its good and bad parts. Much of my work is very tedious. But I do like it when we can contribute to figuring out who committed a crime. Well, I'm almost finished here; you can have your bathroom back. I'm going to tape this stall shut with police tape, in case we need to look into it again."

She taped up the stall and packed up her things.

Beverly walked her out the front door. "Thanks for your help. I hope you find something."

"Me too," Jane said. "You just never know what can crack a case."

Chapter Twenty Four

A little later, Beverly remembered there was something she wanted to mention to the officers. She hoped they hadn't left yet. She hustled out to the parking lot to see if their car was still there. They were just leaving, and she was able to catch them as Mike and Jim were walking out to their car. Beverly said,

"Jim, Mike, I forgot to let you know that I'm changing my schedule a little." The three stopped for a moment near the front door of the senior center. Beverly noted that the rain had stopped, but it was still gray. Just then, they were stopped by Bill, one of the seniors, a man who looked to be in his eighties with unnaturally dark hair and a mustache. He'd been smoking a cigar away from the building. He crushed his cigar on the ground, picked it up and threw it in the trash can.

"Hi, Bill," Beverly said. "How's it going?"

"Beverly, I remembered something that I'd forgotten the day of the murder."

He turned to the officers and said, "I was there the day the janitor was killed."

He pointed to Mike, "I talked with you that day."

Mike said, "Yes, of course. I remember talking with you."

"Well, when we finished our conversation, you said to call if I remembered anything else. And I did remember something today."

"Do you want to go inside?"

"Nah, I'd rather sit in your squad car if you don't mind. They're kind of neat."

Mike said smiling, "Sounds like you may have had some experience sitting in squad cars."

"Oh, I did once. Something about driving without a license or some drivel like that."

"Ah,"

Jim and Mike looked at each other as they escorted Bill to the curb where they had parked the squad car. Mike opened up the back door of the car, and Bill slid inside. Beverly slipped in next to him. The officers got into the front, and Jim took out his notebook.

Jim said, "What would you like to talk with us about, Bill?"

"Well, it's funny how your memory works, especially when you get older. I didn't remember something that happened that very morning. But then it came to me this morning."

Jim looked at him expectantly.

Bill continued, "Tuesday morning I got to the center early, at about seven fifteen. I can usually get a nice cup of coffee and some conversation at that time of the morning. Well, I sat down with my coffee, and then I had to go to the bathroom." He shook his head, "I feel like I have to go to the bathroom all the time."

The three sat patiently and let him ramble a bit about the state of his prostate.

"Anyway, when I was going into the bathroom, I heard two people arguing. Not one to miss out, I stayed quietly by the door but didn't go in. Well, I was able to make out the voices. It was the janitor and Paul, the director."

Mike asked, "Do you remember what they said to each other?"

"Most of it was muffled. My ears aren't as good as they used to be. But they were talking about money. I know that. I think Joe was wanting more money, no, more like they were talking about money. I know that. I think Joe was wanting more money—demanding more money.

"Now I thought that was kind of unusual. I know I've asked my bosses for raises in the past, but that's sure not the right way to go about it. So I don't think they were discussing Joe's pay, if you know what I mean. I seemed like they were talking about hush money or something."

"Hush money? Why do you say that?" Jim asked.

"There was a lot of anger in both of their voices."

"Is there anything else you remembered, like, where the voices were coming from?" Mike asked.

"They must have been standing in the hall, around the corner from the men's room because when I opened the rest room door—I couldn't wait any longer—the voices stopped abruptly. That's all I remember."

Mike said, "Thank you so much for your help, Bill. We'll look into this."

Bill looked at Mike, then Jim, "Now is there anything you boys can do to get my driver's license reinstated?"

They looked at each other and rolled their eyes.

Jim said, "You know Bill, as much as we'd like to help you there, it's really not our area. You'll have to go to the DMV for that. We're homicide detectives."

Bill smiled, showing his gold front tooth, "Well, it was worth a shot!"

With that, Jim opened up the back door and Bill and got out.

Chapter Twenty Five

Beverly stayed in the squad car. She definitely wanted to hear what they said about Paul and the argument.

Mike looked over to Jim and said, "When would be the best time to question Paul again? Probably the sooner the better."

Jim's cell phone rang. He picked it up, "Jim Swenson."

Mike and Beverly listened to the conversation from one side.

"Oh hi, what's up?"

"Really? Well I'd really like to talk with him. Give me his number, I'll call him right now." He jotted down a number.

"OK, bye, and thanks."

Mike asked, "Who was that?"

"That was my sister-in-law, you know, my brother's wife? Anyway, her father goes to the senior center a lot, and he said he'd poke around a bit. She said he's all excited, that he may have some important information for our case."

"Just what we need, another amateur detective," Mike said.

Beverly glared at him and said, "Amateur detective, huh? Is that what you think of me?"

Mike turned red and said, "Oh no, that's not what I meant."

Jim said, "I figured it can't hurt to listen to the guy ramble a little. I'll call him and put him on speaker phone. We can take notes. His name is James Knox. Do you know him, Beverly?"

"Hmm," she said, tapping her nails on the bars between herself and the front seat. "Oh, yes, now I remember him. He's been coming to the center for a while. He's a nice man. Not a big talker. I think he's a retired principal."

Jim put the phone on speakerphone and called James Knox.

After his hellos, James said, "I just want you to know, I'm not the gossiping type. I leave that to my wife," he said with a chuckle.

"But I did hear something about one of the seniors that I thought might be helpful to you."

"What did you hear?" Jim asked.

"Well, I guess that janitor had offended a number of people in general, but mostly Jewish people. I'm sure you've heard about what he said to Laura Goldstein, right?"

"Yes."

"Well, there's a fellow who started coming to the center recently. His name is Nathan Small. He had heard through a friend about this janitor, and he got really upset about it. I heard that he started coming to the center specifically to check him out."

"I can understand that it would be very offensive to anyone when someone makes those types of comments," Jim said.

"But that's not the whole story. Nathan was a Holocaust survivor. He was just a young teen when he was separated from his parents and grandparents. His whole family was sent to death camps. He was lucky to survive because he was rather young. Usually, the youngsters were automatically killed, since they couldn't do much work. Anyhow, he had to say goodbye to his family and was sent on a train to a work camp for the rest of the war. He endured horrible conditions, and because of the shock of losing his family, he has never really healed."

"That's awful," Jim replied.

"Well, after the war he went to Israel and was adopted by a family there. He became very interested in keeping the Holocaust remembered and spent his whole life fighting Nazis. You know, there are a fair number of neo-Nazis here, even in liberal Portland."

"Yes, I know, we've had a few dealings with them. They're a hateful group," Jim said.

"Anyway, it's been his life's passion to make sure that the way his family died was never forgotten."

"I can certainly understand that. Do you know if Nathan was part of an organization?"

"That I don't know. But I do know that he's very charming, and everyone at the center likes him very much. I personally have never been to any of the dances, but I hear he's a great dancer and all the ladies just love him."

"I've heard that too. But in your opinion, do you think he could be violent?"

"You know, Jim. I've seen a lot of things in my day, so nothing surprises me anymore. I think that seeing your whole family go off to be annihilated, especially at such a young age, has got to leave a very deep impact."

"Is there anything else you think I should know?"

"Well, as I said, I'm not prone to gossip, but it wouldn't surprise me if other people wanted to help him in his quest. Maybe cover for him, protect him—that type thing. You have to remember that many of these seniors lived through the horror of that war and its aftermath."

"Yes, you're right. Thank you, James. I think this information will prove to be very helpful in our investigation."

"I'm happy to help. Now you let me know if there's anything else you want me to do."

"I will. Thanks again," Jim said, and hung up.

Mike looked at him and raised one eyebrow.

Beverly piped up, "I think we may have a motive."

Beverly went back into the center after getting out of the police car. She checked on Jane the technician.

"I'm just about done here," Jane said.

After she was completely finished, Beverly showed her out and went back to her office and created a list of events from memory.

I feel like something is missing here, but I can't put my finger on it. Maybe Jane found something of value. It just doesn't add up, she thought. Then, she remembered that she had to finish cleaning the ladies room. She walked out of her office, then almost as an afterthought went back, got her key ring and locked her office door. She went back to the ladies room. She had left her supply caddie on the floor and was glad that nobody tripped over it. She picked it up and cleaned up the toilets, then worked on the sinks and countertop. After cleaning the mirror, she lugged over the heavy mop and started mopping the floor. Just then Tilly came in.

"Hi Tilly, it's just me," Beverly said. "I haven't mopped much of the floor yet. Come on in. Just watch your step under the third sink there."

"Oh, I'm glad it's you in here and not a man. I don't believe I could have held it," She went to the bathroom and then came out and started washing her hands while Beverly waited to resume her mopping. "Looks like you're going to need to fill up the soap dispenser soon, dear."

"OK, I'll make a mental note of it."

"Good thing you're young! I can't remember a thing I need to do unless I write it down."

"Don't you have to get back to the bridge game?" Beverly said, knowing that Tilly was well known for her bridge prowess.

"We're taking a twenty-minute break between sessions."

"I better hold off on the mopping, then. There may be more women needing to use the facilities." She took off her rubber gloves and washed her hands. "I wanted to go out there and chat for a while and have a cup of coffee anyway."

So they walked together.

"Say Tilly, were you aware of Kat's situation with her son a couple months back?"

"Oh, yes. That was awful for Kat. I felt so bad for her. Can you imagine what that would be like to have your own flesh and blood stalking you?"

"I don't know if this is true, but I heard that Kat disowned him and took him out of her will."

"Yes, and he was pretty ticked off about it."

"Did he stand to inherit a lot of money?"

"You don't know about Kat, do you?"

"I guess not. What's her story?"

"Kat's husband Samuel was a brilliant engineer. He died about five years ago. Toward the end of his career, he invented something. I'm not sure what it was—it didn't make sense when Kat explained it to me—some part that goes into computers. Well, he started his own company and marketed that product for a while, and then one of the big high-tech companies bought his company. I can't remember which company it was. Anyway, the big company bought Samuel's firm for over three million dollars."

"Wow! I never knew. Even though she dresses nice and all, Kat doesn't strike me as particularly wealthy or anything."

"I think she lives much like she lived before the buyout. She even told me that she still clips coupons. Heck, she could probably buy the whole grocery store if she wanted to." Tilly said. "I better get back to my bridge table. See you later, Beverly."

"Oh Tilly, just one quick question: what is Kat's son's name?"

"Samuel Jr. He was named after Kat's husband."

"Thanks. Good luck with your game today."

"Honey, when you're as good as me, you don't need luck," she smiled and winked.

Beverly waved goodbye to Tilly and slowly made her way up to the counter to get some coffee. She thought to herself, *Three million dollars! That would make anyone crazy.* She glanced over at Kat, who was at Tilly's bridge table. She was smiling, shuffling the cards. Who'd have ever thought?

Beverly added some cream and sugar to her coffee and went to sit down at a half-empty table. She talked with a few people, then saw that the progressive party-bridge game started up again, and she decided to finish up her mopping. She headed back to the ladies room and finished the mopping, then put a "Caution, Wet Floor" plastic sign that had been hooked on to the bucket on the floor outside of the restroom and propped the door open.

She headed back to the supply cabinet and put everything away. She grabbed a few rolls of toilet paper and paper towels and headed back to the men's room to fill up the dispensers. She wanted to fill up the women's room dispensers, but remembered that the floor was still wet, so she just went back to her office with the supplies and stuck them on her desk to remind her to do it later.

She decided to check in with Paul. She walked down the hallway to his office and even though his door was open, she knocked on the door and saw that he wasn't on the phone, so she popped her head in.

"Hi, Paul. How's your day going?"

"It's going OK. I've been trying to call the district office to get the necessary forms to open up a requisition for the custodial position, but I keep getting the runaround. I'm hoping that they have the forms on the web page. I've been looking for them, but it's a pretty disorganized site."

"Oh," Beverly said, "I think I might remember where it is. Can I check on your computer?"

"Sure, go right ahead, I'm not having any luck."

He stood up and let Beverly have his chair. He sat on his visitor's chair. She noticed again that his office was a bit larger than Beverly's, but like Beverly's, it was strictly government issued issue—ugly metal desk, uncomfortable chairs, standard issue supplies. But Paul had brought in some colorful framed prints that covered the walls. Big, bold prints of abstract paintings. It added a lot of character to the room. And he had brought a few things from home, like a fancy leather desk set with a blotter pad covering the stained metal desktop. Beverly thought that she might do something like that to her blah office, but then remembered that she was on a strict budget with no money for fancy desk sets and prints.

Beverly was secretly looking around his office, looking for clues. She didn't really know what she was looking for. She dropped her pen on purpose and looked under his desk. No luck; nothing. She got up and put her attention back on the computer screen.

"Here you go. Got it! These forms were really buried on the website."

Paul stood behind her and looked at the forms. "Beverly, what would I do without you?"

"Well, for one thing, you'd have to clean the toilets yourself!"

Chapter Twenty Six

After helping Paul find the forms that he needed, Beverly headed back to her office. She wanted to call Jim to let him know the amount of money that Kat's son lost when his mother changed her will. She speed dialed him.

"Jim Swenson here," he said gruffly.

"Hi, Jim. I just found some more information about Kat Orton. She was the woman whose son was stalking her. Remember her?"

"Yes," she heard him shuffling papers. "You said that Kat had disowned him and took him out of the will, right?"

"Yes. Well, I just found out how much money we're talking about. Her deceased husband was an engineer, and he invented something that went into computers. He had his own company, and one of the high tech companies bought him out for three million dollars. Kat is a millionaire!"

Jim whistled, "Well, although people murder for a pork chop, that's a lot of money."

"A pork chop? There's got to be a story there."

"One of the detectives on the force is a former Chicago cop. He told me about a couple brothers who were fighting over the last pork chop on the plate one evening at dinnertime. This happened about twenty years ago or so. Well, the one brother took the last pork chop, and the other brother stabbed him to death."

"Unbelievable!"

"You'd be amazed at the stuff we see and hear about. Anyway, that's very good information you found out about Kat. Did you happen to get the son's name? I'd like to run a check on him."

"His name is Samuel Orton. Samuel Jr. He's named after his dad. And is there any way to see if he's related to Terri Orton?

She's the copy-machine salesperson that met with me that day. Orton seems like an unusual name."

"Yes, I'll get that information," he said.

Beverly said, "But then what about the murder of the woman, Bethany? If it was Samuel Orton who killed Joe, then we've lost the Nazi connection."

"That would appear to be the case. But things aren't always as they seem."

"Unless, well—what if Orton had been stalking Joe for a while and knew that he was friends with Bethany? Maybe he was trying to make it look like there was a connection there but there really wasn't."

"It's possible." Jim said.

"It just almost seems too easy—the Nazi-fighter angle. Don't you think?"

"I'm not sure. I need to talk with everyone involved," he said. "Was there anything else you uncovered?"

"No, I think I've briefed you on everything—briefed you, that's a detective term, isn't it? Aren't I becoming quite the professional?" she said.

"Yes. If I could, I would hire you as a detective," he laughed. "But I warn you, it's not all it's cracked up to be. It can be very tedious, but it is rewarding when we catch who did it."

"That's exactly what your CSI technician said. Well, go to it." Beverly said, "I know I'm not an official detective, but I would very much like to know what happens here."

"I'll tell you as much as I can. You have to understand that for official reasons it generally isn't everything."

"Oh, I understand. I'll talk with you soon." she said, and they hung up.

Chapter Twenty Seven

Beverly was at work, but her mind was on the murders. She mused over her list of suspects. Would it be someone obvious? Did she even have the actual murderer on the suspect list? Maybe it was someone she hadn't even heard of. She really didn't suspect Nathan Small. He was just too trustworthy. And while he had the motive, he just didn't fit the picture. What about Wes and Paul? Blackmailing was a biggie, but something just didn't seem right— why would they kill Bethany in addition to Joe? What did she have to do with it?

But Sam Orton, now that guy was a real nutcase. He had the motive. What did all of the novels say: "follow the money?" But again, why kill Bethany too? It didn't make sense. But still, there was something about that creep.

Beverly heard her cell phone ring and looked at the display. It was Lisa.

"Hi, honey," she said.

"Hi, Mom, I've decided to come home now, tonight. I'm all packed up and ready to go."

"Are you sure you're up for it? Why don't you get an early start tomorrow when you're fresher?"

"Don't be such a worry wart. I took a really long nap this afternoon. I feel fine."

"Well just remember, it's a three-hour trip. Make sure you take lots of breaks. When I was pregnant with you, it seemed like my back was always sore and I had to go to the bathroom all the time."

"My back is fine, but I do have some queasiness in the mornings. That's part of the reason I'd rather make the drive now instead of in the morning."

"Well, just be careful. Do you still have that emergency pack that I put in your trunk?" she was referring to a large package of various items, including emergency water and granola bars.

"Yes, Mom. I'm off!"

"Call me from the road, OK?"

"I sure will, Mom. See you in about three hours."

Beverly checked her watch: four thirty. So Lisa should be home about seven thirty or so. That was good because it would still be light outside. But Beverly hoped Lisa would take a few breaks along the way, so that would put her in closer to eight. *I'll be home by then.* She nodded to herself. *I better stop at the store and pick up a few things.* She dug through her purse and found the list she had started earlier in the week. *So much has changed since I started this list!* she thought as she noticed that Paul walked by.

He stepped into her office, "Are you OK closing up Beverly? There are three volunteers in the kitchen area; they plan to stay until closing."

"Sure, no problem. I'll lock up at about six. And Lisa's coming home from school tonight. I can't wait to see her."

"Isn't it the middle of the semester?" he asked.

"Oh, I guess I didn't tell you the latest," she said and then filled him in on Lisa's woes.

He made the appropriate sympathetic groans and "tsks" then said, "Wes and I are celebrating our two-year anniversary tonight. I can't believe it's been two years already. See you tomorrow. You're opening up, right?"

"Yes, I guess I am. Give my best to Wes. I'll be in at seven tomorrow. So no rush. Don't bother to get here early."

Paul waved goodbye and walked away.

It was five forty five by the time Beverly finished up her paperwork and went over to the kitchen after locking up her office. There were three volunteers there, including Emily, straightening up the kitchen. Beverly washed her hands and helped put the freshly washed dishes away. A few years back, the center had purchased a new industrial-size dishwasher. Beverly remembered that it had taken a lot of negotiating to get the money to buy it, but she was really glad that she'd made the effort. The dishes were done in minutes, it was so easy. Beverly and all of the kitchen volunteers had special food-preparation training, and their kitchen was certified as meeting the health-department guidelines. When they completed their clean up tasks, the ladies put their aprons in the dirty-clothes basket that was filling up fast since Joe was gone, got their purses from the back kitchen storage room, and got ready to leave. It was a warm day, so none of them had coats, although most had sweaters that they put on. The four of them marched out and waited for Beverly to lock up the kitchen area, then they went out the door and the volunteers went to their cars while Beverly locked up the building.

"Thanks so much for your help, ladies!" she said, waving to them.

They all said "You're welcome," to her and went on their way.

Beverly drove straight to the grocery store and conducted a major shopping expedition, chastising herself for shopping on an empty stomach. She picked up many of Lisa's favorite foods and then realized that her daughter may have totally different tastes now, being pregnant. She put two boxes of saltine crackers, a bag of ginger snaps, and three two-liter bottles of ginger ale into her cart. After she was done, she wheeled her cart up to the front. The cart had one bum wheel that kept spinning around, making it hard to maneuver. After taking her groceries out and putting them on the belt, the cashier scanned everything. Beverly was shocked when as the cashier calculated the total.

"A hundred and fifty dollars! I haven't spent that much on groceries in a long time." she said to the cashier, whom she recognized.

"Are you having a party or something?" she asked.

"No, but my daughter is coming home from college."

"I know how that is. You need to stock up for that. Do you need help out?"

"No thanks."

"Well, have a good day," said the cashier with a big smile.

Beverly went out to her car and loaded up the trunk. She noted that while the BMW was a really roomy car she had so much junk in her trunk that there wasn't much space left. She even had to put a couple bags onto the floor of the back seat. She drove home and opened up the garage, carefully parking on one side of the driveway instead of pulling into the garage. Last time Lisa was home, she parked right behind her car, and Beverly couldn't get out of the garage to get to work, so she had to wake up Lisa to get her car keys and move the car. Beverly wanted to avoid that.

She grabbed a couple bags from her trunk and opened the side door to let herself in. As usual, Scout was there to see her, bubbling with joy.

"Come on outside, Scout, do your business." He happily trotted to the front yard and relieved himself quickly, then was back for more attention. "I have to bring the groceries in Scout, leave me alone for a minute" she said and brought all of the bags in and set them on the kitchen counter.

She quickly put her groceries away, all except the gorgeous rotisserie chicken that she had gotten. She grabbed a plate and a knife and fork, poured herself a glass of chardonnay, and sat at the kitchen table and ate.

"Mmm, this is so good." she said. "But sorry, Scout, you can't have any. You'll get your kibble in a minute." She got up and pushed the button to close the garage door. "I can't wait for Lisa to come. You met her when she was home for spring break, remember Lisa?" Scout thumped his tail. "You don't know what I'm talking about, do you Scout?" He thumped his tail even harder in reply. She laughed and finished up eating her fill. She put the plastic cover back on the chicken and put it in the fridge.

"Ah, that fridge looks nice and full now, doesn't it, Scout?" she said, rinsing off her plate and putting it in the dishwasher. "Well Mr. Patient, here's your dinner," she said, scooping out his food and making him sit, then giving him the OK.

He devoured his dinner while Beverly finished cleaning up, pondering her future: no Herb, dead end job, adult daughter coming back home, grandchild on the way...

Chapter Twenty Eight

Later that evening, Beverly looked at her watch: seven thirty. *Ah, now I can relax,* she said to herself. She felt it was warm enough outside so she opened up all the windows and sliding back door to let some fresh air in. She put fresh sheets on Lisa's bed and tried to straighten up a little. She poured herself another glass of wine and sat down with an Agatha Christie mystery that she never seemed to have the time to get through.

"I should have about half an hour or so before Lisa gets here, Scout," she said and sat in her comfy chair in the living room where she'd be able to see Lisa's car drive up.

As she sat and waited, she thought more about the murders. She decided to talk it over with Scout, since he was such a good listener.

"That Sam Orton gives me the creeps," she said, as Scout looked up at her. "He definitely had the motive—money is really big. And he had the opportunity. Shoot, he's probably been stalking Joe for some time. Yes—that must be how he knew Joe was friends with Bethany," she said and stood up.

Then she sat back down, "And he killed her to throw the investigation toward the neo-Nazi angle. He probably knew about Joe's anti-Semitism and his remarks to the seniors. I think he did it! I would bet money on it!"

She heard something and stood up. "Oh, she must be here early!" she said, nearly knocking over her wine. Scout started barking, unsure where the sound was coming from. Beverly looked out the front window but didn't see Lisa's car. "It's probably nothing. Calm down, Scout." But Scout ran to the back sliding door.

A man was standing at the back sliding door, and he slid open the door and came into house.

Beverly screamed as she looked at the tall, muscle-bound man. She recognized him as Kat's Orton's son Sam, whom she was just thinking about. And he had a gun pointed right at her. His dark eyes looked glassy, and they were looking straight into her eyes.

"What are you doing here? Get out!" she exclaimed, shocked and afraid.

Scout, sensing the danger, ran over to the man with his mouth open, lips back, preparing for attack. Beverly saw his raised hackles.

Sam yelled, "Get that idiot dog away from me or I'll shoot it!"

With the strength that came from fear, Beverly grabbed Scout's collar and struggled to pull him away from the man. The dog was very strong and resisted. He started growling at Sam, but Beverly persisted.

"Now lock him up."

Beverly thought fast. She was trying to remember where her cell phone was. It was upstairs in her bedroom, buried in her purse somewhere.

"I'll just put him upstairs, and then he won't bother us."

"No I don't think so," he sneered. "Put him right in that room," pointing to the closest room—the laundry room, "And don't try anything. I'm right behind you with the gun pointed right at your heart."

The blood was pounding in her ears as she closed Scout in the laundry room, glad that the window was open and hoping that a neighbor might hear his barking and be alerted. Scout continued barking and crying and scratching the door.

Sam nudged Beverly back to the family room and said, "Now, what do we have here?"

Beverly looked at him, thinking that the best thing to do was to keep him talking. After all, he had a gun.

"Your name's Beverly, isn't it?" he said.

"Yes."

"Of course, you work at the senior center, don't you?"

"Yes, you're Kat's son, aren't you?"

"You would know that!" he said loudly. "You told me to leave, didn't you?"

"I do remember doing that. But you were really scaring your mother."

"She should be scared, the old bat! She's going to leave all my money to charity. To charity! Three million dollars, probably more by now, the cheapskate doesn't spend a dime. It should be mine."

"Why are you here? What do I have to do with it?"

"Well, maybe you should answer that, little miss nosey-pants."

"What do you mean?" Beverly said, glancing at her watch: seven fifty. She was afraid her daughter would come soon and be in danger. She had to think of something.

"What do you mean?" he said, mockingly. "You told that Joe guy to throw me out, didn't you? And I was just trying to change my mother's mind about me. And he punched me in the face."

"Was that any reason to kill him?"

"Is there a better one?" he asked, his eyes looking even more glazed.

"How'd you do it?" she asked.

He continued pointing the gun at her heart as she looked at him, shaking. "I guess I can tell you, since you'll be dead soon too. And your little dog too!" He cackled like the witch in the *Wizard of Oz*.

"It was a pretty good plan, if I do say so myself. I got to know the layout of the place just by going to see my mother there. So I knew all the hallways and where the keys were kept. You really have shit security there, you know."

Beverly knew she needed to keep him talking if she had any chance of survival, but at the same time she didn't want Lisa to come home until after he was gone. She was torn.

"Yes, that's true. Last year, I got some bids for a security system for the center, but we never did get funding. I was angry because I put a lot of effort into it, and so did the vendors." She was rambling.

"Shut up! I don't want to hear about the stupid security system."

"Well, how did you do it? It was really a good plan I think," she stammered.

"So I had it all planned out. I slipped in early in the morning that day and waited. I knew that my wife was going to distract you and that pansy director of yours."

"Terri Orton is your wife?"

"Yes, she is. She was in on it too." Beverly was truly shocked. "I waited until I knew that she'd be talking to you and that director, then a made a little commotion down the hallway where I knew Joe was. Then I hid around the corner and hit him from behind. I bashed him up real good with this pipe. It was great to hear the smack when he hit the ground. But he was still alive. So I had to use my backup plan. I just pulled out my knife and stabbed him in the back."

"What did you do with the pipe?"

"I was in a hurry you know. I hid it under one of the classroom tables. And you know what? I remembered to pick it up the next day, wearing gloves of course. You guys really should get better locks put on those windows. And I put it in one of the toilets. In the ladies room. Wasn't that brilliant?"

"How did you get out of the center after you killed him?"

"That's what was so great. I just walked out the front door, plain as day. None of those old biddies even noticed me."

"But what about Joe's friend, that woman with the black hair? What did she have to do with it? Why'd you kill her too?"

"Oh, I knew all about her. I'd been watching Joe for quite some time. I knew he had that Nazi symbol on his back. I'd seen the outline of it one time when I was watching him. He was wearing a white t-shirt at the time. And I saw that his girlfriend had one too."

Then the phone rang and Scout resumed his loud barking.

"Don't answer it," he said loudly. She looked at the caller ID.

"But it's my daughter." she said, thinking fast. "I have to pick up because this is our regular calling time. She'll be suspicious and start calling emergency numbers if I don't answer."

He paused a moment, then said, "OK, pick it up. But don't try anything." He continued pointing the gun at her chest.

"Hello, honey," she said.

"Hi, Mom, I just wanted to let you know that I'm ten minutes away, right by the grocery store. Do you want me to pick something up? And why is Scout barking so much?"

While Lisa was talking, Beverly was frantically thinking of how to send her a message that she needed help. Then she remembered the code that they used when Lisa was in high school.

"You know, I'd love to see you, but I'm so tired that I just want a nap."

"What? Do we have a bad connection or something? I just wanted to know if you need anything from the grocery store."

"No, don't bother coming over. I'm just so tired that I'm going to take a nap."

"Oh my god, Mom, our code! You're in trouble aren't you?"

"Yes, I'm so tired."

"I'll call 911." She hung up.

"Yes dear, I think it would be better if you didn't come over tonight. Why don't you give me a call tomorrow, OK? We'll get together then," she paused. "Goodbye Lisa. I love you," she said and hung up.

"Oh, how sweet, you love your daughter don't you? My mother doesn't love me. Or else she would still leave me the money that I deserve."

"You were telling me about the girl—you know, Joe's friend."

"Yeah, the one with the half cut-off hair. She had a Nazi symbol tattoo also. Did you know that?"

"Oh really?"

"Well, I knew that the cops would look at me if Joe was killed, but it would be considered a whole 'reverse hate crime' thing if I took her out too. So I waited and watched her. She was so predictable, so easy. I knew where she lived and what she did. So I just followed her to the grocery store and got her from behind before she even went in. Then I dragged her to the back of the lot where she wouldn't be found for a while."

"Well, I'm sure you were right about that. I'm sure those cops were fooled real good."

"I think that was the best part of my plan."

Beverly wasn't sure, but she thought she heard some faint sirens getting a little louder and louder. She hoped and prayed that someone was coming.

"But how did you kill her? I didn't find out. Did you stab her too?"

"No dammit, I left my good knife inside that jerk, Joe."

"Oh, right, I forgot about that," Beverly said.

"So I shot her. I shot her twice in the back of the head, just to make sure I got her. She was good and dead when I dragged her across the parking lot."

"But nobody saw you at the parking lot? Seems like there'd be shoppers all the time at the grocery store." She heard the sirens getting louder, then all of the sudden they stopped. Beverly noted that Samuel Orton didn't seem to notice, he was so wrapped up in his story.

"Well, the good part was that the woman only liked to go to the store when it was the least crowded. What's that called? Ago-raphobia or arachnophobia or something like that. I knew this because I'd been watching her. I think she didn't like people or something. So there was really nobody in the lot when I shot her. And I made really quick work of it, getting her across the lot."

Beverly tried to look casual, but she saw activity out her back sliding door. She thought she saw two men slip inside. Yes, she did. They were very quiet, but Scout heard them and started barking wildly again.

"What's the matter with that stupid dog? I think I'm going to just shoot that thing!" he said, and turned toward the laundry room where the dog was locked up.

In that instant, with his gun pointed away, two police officers grabbed Orton as Beverly watched in horror. While Orton was being apprehended Beverly ran out of the family room toward the laundry room. She crouched down and peeked around the corner. She watched as the police wrestled Sam to the ground. Beverly could see that one grabbed Orton's gun and held it up while the other officer continued holding him on the floor. The officer put the gun in his holster and went back to help keep Orton down.

Orton was strong and was thrashing around, but the two police finally got his arms around his back and put handcuffs on him. Sam glared at Beverly, red-faced, and said, "Stupid bitch!"

Beverly started weeping when she saw who the officers were— Officers Swenson and Petrovsky.

"Oh, thank God!" she said, collapsing.

Chapter Twenty Nine

An hour later, Beverly had recovered, but was still shaky. She sat with her daughter by her side and Scout at her feet. She was petting Scout's head absent-mindedly. Orton had been read his rights and taken away, so Beverly, Lisa, and Scout were all alone in the house. They had closed and locked all the windows and doors. Beverly said,

"Oh honey, you saved my life!"

Lisa replied, "No, you saved your own with your quick thinking. I'm just glad I remembered our code.

The phone rang. Lisa picked up. "It's Officer Swenson," she said, handing her mother the phone.

"Hello Jim." Her daughter mouthed "Jim?"

"Yes, you're welcome to come over to take my statement. Come on by."

"See you then. Bye!" and she hung up.

Lisa said, "Jim? You know him by his first name? What's going on?"

"Oh, we've been working together on the murder case. He's the officer in charge, you know. I've been helping him. I bet you didn't know that your mother was an amateur detective?"

"Mom, you surprise me more and more each day. Is he one of the cops from tonight?"

"Yes, the one with the silver hair."

"The hot one? With the bright green eyes? Way to go Mom!"

"I guess he is pretty hot, isn't he? I better get ready," she said, getting up and going upstairs. She freshened up her makeup and hair and came back downstairs. He arrived ten minutes later.

"I don't think I introduced you properly to my daughter yet, Lisa, this is Officer Jim Swenson."

He held out his hand and shook hers.

"You have a really brave mother. She's had quite a week."

"One that I'd just as soon forget. I'm really not that brave. I was just in the wrong place at the wrong time," Beverly said.

"And very good thinking, Lisa, deciphering the code and calling 911 right away."

Lisa replied, "Thanks, I'm just glad I remembered our code."

"Fortunately, Mike and I were on duty when you called in the emergency. We were out in our patrol car and we were really close by. We were shocked that it turned out to be your mom who needed help."

"Well I'll leave you two alone. I know you'll want to take a statement. I'm going to go up to my room and read for a while. It was nice meeting you Officer."

"Please call me Jim."

"OK, Jim," and Lisa went upstairs but gave her mother a big wink before she left. Scout remained at Beverly's feet.

They both started to speak at once.

"You go ahead," Jim said.

"I just don't know how I can thank you and Mike for saving my life."

"Oh no, I'm the one who should be apologizing, the reason he came after you was because he was afraid that you knew too much and that you would figure out his crime. He was a whacko, and I should have been more careful about getting you involved."

"But getting involved with you was fun. Oh wait, I didn't mean it that way," she blushed and laughed. "But I enjoyed detecting. Maybe I can study for a new career."

"But what would all your friends from the center do? You keep that place running, and all the seniors love you!"

"Maybe. I'm sure they'd get along just fine without me."

"Well, I need to take a statement from you, while it's fresh in your mind. But first I need to get something over with." He looked at her. Her stomach did a little flip as she looked into those gorgeous green eyes of his.

She stammered, "What would that ..." and he kissed her.

She really, really enjoyed it, thinking that she hadn't had a kiss like that in a very long time.

"Thank you for letting me do that. I've been wanting to kiss you since about a minute after I met you."

Beverly just stared at him, shocked, but happy.

"Now I can go ahead and take your statement," he said with a heartwarming smile.

On a morning a week after the excitement, Beverly and Lisa got up early and got dressed to go out. Beverly started pacing.

Lisa said, "I better drive. You're a wreck."

After getting into Lisa's car and closing the door, Beverly said, "I don't know why I'm so nervous!"

Lisa said in her most calming voice, "Going back to college is a big step after a long absence. I'm really proud of you."

"It's going to take me years to finish, going part-time," Beverly said.

Lisa countered, "Remember what you used to tell me all the time? When you've got a big project, you just take it one step at a time."

"If I hear that lame salami story again I'll …"

"Take it one slice at a time," Lisa said with a smile.

"But do you think I can handle two night classes at a time? Especially in the summer?" Beverly wailed. "Summer is the best time of year in Portland, and I'm going to miss it!"

"Stop your whining. It'll probably be challenging this summer since the classes are compressed, but the good news is that you'll have two classes over with in no time. And you're not taking super-hard classes first!"

"And then, what if I do all this work and take all these prerequisites and end up not getting accepted into a gerontology program. I'll never be a senior-center or retirement-center director! Geez, I'll *be* a geriatric by the time I'm finally done."

Lisa chuckled, "Then you'll really be able to relate to your clients."

"I feel good about this. And to think it took me so long to figure it out."

"You're fantastic with the seniors at the center. You'll be a natural. And you'll learn so much about the aging process."

"I think it was Myrtle who finally encouraged me to start back at school. Remember her, the volunteer I told you about? The one with more energy than the two of us put together? She finished her college degree when she was in her early eighties. And now she's taking piano lessons—at eighty five"

As they pulled up to the Portland Community College campus, Beverly started rummaging through her purse, "Do you think I have everything I need? Are you feeling OK? No morning sickness today?"

"I'm fine, Mom, and you'll be fine. You'll just need to fill out an application and some more paperwork. Don't worry, it's simple."

"An application? You mean they can reject me? After what happened with your father, I don't think I can handle any more rejection."

"Calm down Mom. They're not going to reject you. You just complete some forms, and later you'll need to request your transcripts."

"Transcripts? You forgot to mention that! You mean from high school? You've got to be kidding! I graduated decades ago! Do they even keep those records that long?" Beverly was wringing her hands in earnest.

"Of course they do," Lisa said with more confidence than she felt. "That's what schools do."

"Do I have to take the SAT test? I hope I don't have to take the SAT test. I don't remember how to measure a triangle. What's that formula?" She scratched her head.

"I doubt you'll have to take the SAT, especially since you've already got a year of college under your belt, but we'll see. Just relax, OK?"

"At least I got good grades in high school, all As and Bs. And my first year of college was good too. Do you think I'll have to take P.E.? I'll flunk if I have to take P.E.!"

"You'll be fine," Lisa said as they got out of the car. She went to the passenger side of her car and grabbed her mother's arm. "Just make sure you study, and you're not distracted by that adorable police officer that's hot for you!"

Beverly blushed, thinking about Jim. They'd had two dates since the incident with Sam, and since Ruth was helping her, things were progressing nicely with her divorce. Ruth assured her that she'd get a decent settlement. She smiled and figured she might be able to cut her work to part-time so she could finish her degree faster. She'd leave the detective work to Jim—she'd had enough of that!

"OK then, let's go!" Beverly said, practically skipping to the admissions office with her daughter.

The End